DR TED CURRUTHERS
&
DR ISAAC STONE

DR TED CURRUTHERS
&
DR ISAAC STONE

Eleanor Berry

The Book Guild Ltd

First published in Great Britain in 2022 by
The Book Guild Ltd
Unit E2 Airfield Business Park,
Harrison Road, Market Harborough,
Leicestershire. LE16 7UL
Tel: 0116 2792299
www.bookguild.co.uk
Email: info@bookguild.co.uk
Twitter: @bookguild

Copyright © 2022 Eleanor Berry

The right of Eleanor Berry to be identified as the author of this
work has been asserted by them in accordance with the
Copyright, Design and Patents Act 1988.

All rights reserved. No part of this publication may be
reproduced, transmitted, or stored in a retrieval system, in any form or by any means,
without permission in writing from the publisher, nor be otherwise circulated in
any form of binding or cover other than that in which it is published and without
a similar condition being imposed on the subsequent purchaser.

This work is entirely fictitious and bears no resemblance to any persons living or dead.

Typeset in 11pt Baskerville

Printed and bound by CPI Group (UK) Ltd, Croydon, CR0 4YY

ISBN 978 1915122 926

British Library Cataloguing in Publication Data.
A catalogue record for this book is available from the British Library.

Introduction

Dr Ted Curruthers was a top Harley Street psychiatrist, who had a consulting room at 113 Harley Street, London, and who had playboy tendencies. He was a clergyman's son who had lost his faith. He had engaging, jagged, white teeth, which delighted women, and lovely, silvery hair. He occupied the same building as a certain Dr Isaac Stone, another top Harley Street psychiatrist. Both were competitive and possessive about their patients, whom they shared. Curruthers was in his sixties, and was quite tall and was profoundly attractive to the majority of his female patients, although he did not know it. He had a cuddly, teddy-bear-look about him.

He had large, brown eyes, which some women referred to as "cow-like" eyes, and a small, but aquiline nose. In general, he looked rather sad, however, and his mien sometimes suggested self-doubt and melancholy behind his smile. Sometimes, he shielded his eyes with dark glasses, which set women's blood on fire.

Some of his female patients liked to run their fingers through his silvery hair. One of them referred to it as "freshly fallen snow on the Steppes of Mother Russia."

Her remark flattered him and made him laugh, showing his jagged, white teeth once more.

His hands were described by his mother as "violinist's hands". Sometimes, they tasted of salt, when the randiest of his female patients licked them.

He wore tight, navy blue trousers, which left nothing to the imagination. The top two buttons of his shirt were permanently undone, and his tie was always loosened at the neck. This was another thing which tended to turn women on in droves, although he seldom noticed their admiration for the way he dressed.

His colleague, Dr Isaac Stone, didn't look like Curruthers in any way, however. He wore heavily striped dark grey suits, which looked so loud, that they could easily have been heard all the way from Algeria. He sported black, Victorian sideburns, which looked ridiculous. These were dyed black, like his hair. His trousers were two sizes too big for him, not unlike a clown's.

One of Ted Curruthers' regular patients was a young woman called Natalie Klein, who hailed from a Welsh family, and like all members of her family, she spoke with a heavy Welsh accent.

Her father, Selwyn Klein, was born in Merthyr Tydfil in South Wales. Selwyn looked similar to the actor, John Wayne, and was famous for his liquid Welsh eyes. He emigrated to London where he became a Tory newspaper proprietor, like his father before him.

"Selwyn Clyndywin" was his father's original surname, but his son changed the name by deed poll to "Klein", because he considered it a simpler name to spell.

All members of the Klein family were literary, in that they had written books at some time during their lives. Natalie's elder sister, Marigold, was an art expert and had written three books about Old Masters. Selwyn had written a number of historical books, before following in his father's footsteps. Natalie's two brothers, Richard and Gomer had written at least six espionage novels between them, and Natalie, herself, had written a large number of black-humoured, gruesome novels which were popular with the general public, as well as with serial killers in prisons.

***

All the members of the Klein family had naturally black hair, except for Natalie, who dyed her hair blonde. She had kept her hair this colour since the age of twenty.

Selwyn's late wife, Elizabeth, died of breast cancer when Natalie was twelve. Elizabeth was extremely eccentric and had a perilously loud voice. She once sat down before a Grace read by the Archbishop of Canterbury.

When she visited Russia, during Stalin's rule, she travelled on the Trans-Siberian Railway, accompanied by an English-speaking guide. She was dissatisfied by the appearance of the endless and monotonous Steppes. "God, this is an ugly country! Oh, this is such an ugly country! Can you *beat* the phenomenal ugliness of this country?" she shouted.

She got off at Vladivostok where she had a man shot.

One summer, after Elizabeth's death, Selwyn and his daughters stayed at a villa in the South of France. It was really hot at the time. Selwyn, Marigold and Natalie, were sitting on the terrace facing the sea, having a *piperade*, served by Selwyn's valet, Jones.

Suddenly, Selwyn fainted and fell backwards onto the flagstones. His appearance was terrifying. His face had become dark-grey, and his eyes were glacial, like those of a dead body. Natalie shook violently, as if she had *Parkinson's Disease*. She was convinced that her father had died. Marigold, her older sister, and by far the most sensible of the two, rushed indoors and sent for a doctor.

Selwyn soon recovered from the fainting attack, but Natalie suffered from post-traumatic stress disorder, which lasted for a few weeks. Selwyn stayed in the villa with his valet, and Marigold booked the two sisters onto a plane bound for Heathrow.

She invited her sister to stay in their family house in Buckinghamshire for a while, but Natalie remained so unwell that she was unable even to write her books, although writing had always been her passion. Indeed, she wrote two books a year on average.

Natalie's Past Life

As is stated in Eleanor Berry's book, *Never Alone With Rex Malone*, Natalie had once been a somewhat thuggish funeral director, who worked in partnership with her beloved Charlie Elliott (deceased). He was a Cornishman, and was born in Looe. Natalie reasoned that no recession could stop people dying.

When her beloved Charlie died, of heart disease, she was so grief-stricken, that she took an overdose, causing her to suffer from horrific hallucinations. She was admitted to St Thomas's Hospital, where the nurses lacked compassion, quite unlike those who looked after the patients, suffering from Coronavirus, at a much later date.

Natalie was convinced that an epidemic of bubonic plague had broken out on the ward she occupied. She was terrified of catching it, so she locked herself in a lavatory for four hours. A male nurse broke the door down, and called her a "fucking whore", which caused Natalie to slap his face. He was sacked within a week.

She had another hallucination and feared that the curtains surrounding the beds were on fire, and called the

Fire Brigade on her mobile. Firemen rushed onto the ward within ten minutes, their hoses ready. When they found out that there was no fire, they too, were very put out, although Natalie told them that the love of her life had just died. She remarked playfully, to add to her sense of black humour, "I have always liked the appearance of firemen, with their earnest faces, and their sweet, little yellow hats."

"Oh, fuck off, you maniac!" said one of the firemen.

"I've just lost the love of my life," repeated Natalie.

"Oh, well, we all have our crosses to bear," said the occupant of the bed next to hers.

"I'll be the first to spit on your fucking husband's grave!" said Natalie.

There was a dying woman in the corner of the ward. A priest was leaning over her bed, giving her the last rites, but Natalie thought the priest was someone coming to make the bed. She asked the priest to come and fix her television.

"Not now I can't. I'm giving last rites at the moment," said the priest patiently.

"I don't care what you're doing. I don't want to miss *Holby City,*" said Natalie.

Natalie had once canvassed for a famous, but controversial politician called Rex Malone, whom she had adulated. (See *Never Alone With Rex Malone*). She had committed a myriad of serious crimes on his behalf, without his knowledge, and as a result had served a custodial sentence. She was released for good behaviour, although the author does not wish to give details.

Natalie's Present Life

After she had been staying in Buckinghamshire with her sister, following her father's fainting attack, Natalie stopped taking an interest, either in her food, or in her appearance for a while. She rarely wore make-up or nail-varnish, although she had formerly been vain and particular about her looks. Marigold noticed the deterioration in her sister's vanity, and discussed the matter with Natalie at length. The two sisters agreed to seek medical help in London.

The elder sister drove her ailing sister to London, having made an appointment for her to see Dr Sergei Festenstein. He was the much-loved G.P. of the Klein family, and occupied rooms close to 113 Harley Street.

Dr Festenstein was a Jewish refugee from Leipzig. He and his wife, Berthe, had only just managed to escape from the Nazis. He spoke English with a guttural Leipzig accent, which turned his female patients on like lights.

Berthe was envious of these women, and frequently sat in the hall, leading to her husband's consulting room. Her jealousy was understandable. He had a charming smile and a mischievous twinkle in his eyes, which were often focussed on women. He had thick, predominantly dark hair, which was streaked with grey. In addition, the whites of his eyes were reddish. This unusual feature also attracted women.

His initials, S.F. were embroidered on his ties, and he wore Saville Row suits, which were meticulously chosen by his wife. He had looked after the Klein family since Natalie was four. Like many of his female patients, she found him ravishing, ever since the age of about fourteen, when she began to flirt outrageously with him. Although he enjoyed her advances, he pretended to ignore them.

***

The Klein sisters were ushered into his consulting room by a receptionist, and Dr Festenstein, who was sitting behind a large, leather desk, invited them to sit in magenta armchairs. "Sit down, my children," said Festenstein. The doctor looked at the note which Marigold had written to him before setting out. He knew about Selwyn's tendency to faint and was aware how frightening a fainting attack could appear to someone who hadn't witnessed one before.

"I've got just the fellow for you, little Natalie," he said. "Apparently, he knows you well. You've seen him before. His name is Dr Ted Curruthers. He was present at your beloved Charlie's funeral." Dr Festenstein wrote a short letter addressed to Dr Curruthers, and put it into a sealed envelope.

"Dr Curruthers has rooms at 113 Harley Street. Take this letter to him little one. He's a close friend and colleague of mine. We often have lunch together. Try not to flirt with him. I know you will, because he's so handsome. Keep your sister out of mischief, won't you, Marigold."

The sisters thanked the doctor and left, after Marigold had paid the bill. She hailed a black cab and was about to get into it.

"I would prefer to go alone," said Natalie unexpectedly.

"That doesn't sound like you."

"It's what I want."

"OK, I'll go and get my nails done. Then I'll meet you at 113 Harley Street, after your appointment," said Marigold.

"Where to?" asked the taxi-driver tersely. It was obvious that he was in a bad mood.

Natalie leant forward and pressed her face against the glass partition, dividing her from the driver.

"113 Harley Street, please, driver."

"That's not at all far from here, Lady. Can't you go there on foot?"

"No, I can't. I've just had a hip operation," lied Natalie aggressively, adding, "I'd rather you drove me the whole way there, and kindly refrain from addressing me as, 'Lady'."

Natalie was dressed smartly that day. She was wearing a velvet leopard-skin suit. Leopard skin was her favourite pattern and her choice of clothing suggested that she may well have been feeling better.

She paid the bill but refused to tip the driver. She got out of the cab and deliberately failed to close the door behind her. She rang the bell, outside 113 Harley Street, and the door opened automatically. A receptionist, aged about fifty-five, led her along the corridor, to the ground floor waiting room, where both Curruthers and Stone met their patients.

The incensed cab-driver turned off his ignition, and banged his fist on the dashboard. He stormed round to the back of his cab, and made a v-sign at Natalie. She gave him an artificial smile, from the end of the corridor.

"Thank you so much for your chivalry, my good man!" she called out, loudly enough for him to hear her voice. She had a very loud voice which she had inherited from her mother.

Curruthers came into the waiting room, within five minutes. He was wearing his customary tight trousers, with the top two buttons of his shirt undone, and his tie loosened at the neck. This turned Natalie on like a light.

She observed his thick, silvery hair and his sad, brown eyes. Despite the terror she had experienced when her father had fainted, she rapidly forgot the worst of her trauma. Her exhibitionist streak came into its own, and she failed to mince her words.

"God, you look sexy! Do you have a lot of mistresses?" she asked him precociously.

"Natalie, really!" he replied. He smiled at her. "We'll have to go up to the fourth floor in the antiquated lift, I'm afraid. My rooms are on the fourth floor."

"I don't mind. Would there be any chance of our bodies touching each other, once we got into the lift?"

"No comment!" replied Curruthers. He tried to keep a straight face and held the door of the lift open for Natalie. It only held about three people. Natalie looked lecherously at the doctor's brown eyes, and tight trousers.

"May I call you "Ted," she asked.

"I don't see why not."

She tried to unzip his flies. The zip was very stiff.

"Naughty! Basket!" he said. He sounded like someone speaking to a dog.

"There is no basket here, but, speaking figuratively, how can I possibly get into my basket, when my hand and eyes are telling me you are almost in a state of readiness?" said Natalie. "Please get it out. I think I'll go mad if you don't!" she added vulgarly.

It didn't take him long to become hard, so hard that she could barely get his cock into her mouth. She licked it hungrily, almost biting it. He stared vacantly into space.

The lift stopped on the second floor. A fairly short man got into it. This was Dr Isaac Stone. He was about fifty-five and looked very embarrassed.

While Natalie was fellating Curruthers, Stone stared at his unpolished shoes and tried to remember where he had bought them. He was irritated because his valet had failed to polish them recently. He desperately needed a scapegoat.

"Dash it all, Curruthers! I feel this is letting down the street," he said mildly, adding, "can't you ever do your tie up properly?" He spoke with an upper-class accent, which had a slight Belfast lilt, as if he had spent time in Northern Ireland.

"Many women like it when I wear my tie like this," said Curruthers. He was unable to prevent himself from panting loudly. Eventually, he ejaculated into the palm of his hand, rather than down Natalie's throat, for he was a gentleman. Natalie lowered her head and smiled furtively at him and winked at him.

Curruthers managed to recover his breath, and put his cock back into his flies. He stared vacantly into space once more, while Natalie did the same. Stone continued to look at his shoes, and thought seriously about sacking his valet.

Curruthers stared Stone in the eye.

"I haven't mentioned this before," he began. "I am a clergyman's son, and I have been brought up not to pass personal remarks. However, your suits are so bloody loud, that they can be heard all the way from Algeria!"

Stone was very proud and he resented anyone who criticised his appearance, with which he invariably took considerable trouble. Also, he had received a trenchant letter from his bank manager that morning, in which he had been told that he would not be granted another overdraft facility. He was even more furious with his colleague, however, and resented his exhibitionist behaviour. On reaching the next floor, he wrenched the door of the lift open, causing one of his long, manicured fingernails to snap off.

He dragged Curruthers by the collar, as best he could, pushed him towards the black-and-white-check-tiled landing, of which there are many in Harley Street, and gave him a resounding slap on the ear. A scruffy-looking cleaner, with her hair in curlers, staggered on to the landing. She was carrying a mop and bumper, which were obviously too heavy for her, and glared at the two psychiatrists, both of whom she knew well.

"All them doctors, they're just like a load of bleedin' old apple women!" she muttered with a heavy southern Irish accent.

"Perhaps, it would be better to sort all this out in the street," suggested the bemused clergyman's son. He spoke forcefully, betraying a trace of a south London lilt, which was curiously mixed with an Etonian twang. His south London lilt was artificial and affected, to relax some of his less upper-class patients.

Curruthers and Stone failed to notice Natalie, who had been following them onto the pavement. She had always been turned on by stories about men fighting and films of the same. At first, the two psychiatrists fought like a couple of cowboys from the wild west. Stone was so anxious not to damage his unusually crude-looking suit, that he was more sparing with the delivery of his blows, than his opponent.

Dr Curruthers recalled seeing Natalie before, at Charlie's cremation service in North London. He remembered being particularly moved when she had bounded forward, as the curtains were closing, at the end of the ceremony, in an attempt to gain access to the coffin on its way to the flames.

"My G.P., Dr Festenstein, has specifically referred me to you," she ventured, as the fight came to a close. "I've got a letter from him, addressed to you, Dr Curruthers, although you did say I could call you 'Ted', didn't you?"

"Yes, of course, Natalie."

Stone was averse to fighting on pavements, particularly those in Harley Street. He brushed his suit fastidiously, as if it were his only possession. He appeared rather self-conscious and glanced briefly at the building, which he entered via the staircase, his head lowered and his icy-looking eyes almost crossing each other.

Marigold was in the waiting room, expecting to find her sister.

"I'm waiting for my sister," she said.

"I don't know who you are, so I have no idea who your sister is either," said Stone irritably.

"Her name's Natalie Klein. She came to see Dr Curruthers."

"No doubt she'll be ready to leave shortly."

Natalie joined her sister within about ten minutes, she was looking unnaturally flushed and contented.

Natalie saw Ted in his fourth-floor consulting room every Tuesday afternoon. It had not taken her long to recover from her father's fainting attack. Selwyn paid the bills and Natalie told him that she had been suffering from depression.

"When are you going to fuck me?" she asked Ted coarsely after one of the sessions. "We've been seeing each other for quite some time now."

"If I were to do that, I could lose my house, my family and my livelihood. In fact, I could be struck off the register altogether."

Natalie ignored his statement.

"Where do you live?" she asked.

"Hampstead."

"I still don't understand why we can't go to bed together, say, to a hotel. No one would find out."

"We just can't, Natalie. You'd be surprised how word gets round, particularly in Harley Street," said Ted.

"If we were to go to a hotel, no one in Harley Street would find out."

There was a silence. Natalie changed the subject. "Why are your hands always so salty when I lick them?"

"Because I sometimes walk to work in the pouring rain," said Ted.

"What? All the way from Hampstead?"

"No. I often visit the Royal Society of Medicine."

Ted was looking at Natalie's notes. She was sitting in front of him, with her head resting on his knees. He looked cheekily at her, showing his jagged, white teeth once more.

"You've got such lovely teeth," she said. "Incidentally, I heard someone playing the piano in the next-door room just now. Do you usually allow your patients to play, when they are disturbing your consultations?"

Ted smiled, "I only allow them to play, if they play well."

Thereafter, when Natalie met Ted in Harley Street, it was not Ted who cross-examined Natalie, but, at her insistence, it was the other way round.

For some perverse reason, the arrangement excited Ted. Natalie asked him what sort of relationship he had had with his mother, whether he had in any way felt sexually attracted towards his mother, when his first sexual experience had been, and what it had been like. She also asked him when he first started to onanize, and a lot of other intimate questions besides. When she asked him where he had gone to school, he replied that he had been to Eton.

"Were you ever buggered at Eton?" asked Natalie.

"No," Ted replied forcefully.

"Would you have enjoyed it if you had?"

"No, I'm not into fellas."

"What you said was sexually attractive," said Natalie spontaneously.

***

Ted stated that he had been expelled from Eton. When Natalie asked him why, he replied that he had failed to adhere to religious observations in the Eton chapel. He did not recite prayers or sing hymns. Instead, he kept his arms folded, his hands in his pockets and chewed gum loudly.

He was summoned to the headmaster's study, and asked to account for his "subversive" behaviour. He aggressively stated that he no longer believed in a Deity and that he found the obligation to attend chapel services, offensive.

"Before I was expelled, I was made to learn five hundred lines of Virgil, by heart."

"What? In Latin?"

"That's right."

"You showed spirit!" said Natalie. "I don't think you are telling me the truth, though. Don't worry, I have my ways of finding things out, when I am not being told the truth."

"Oh, have you been hiring a private dick?" asked Ted suspiciously. There was a pronounced, paranoid tone in his voice.

"I'm not answering that question. I'll tell you something else, though.

"When my siblings and I were naughty, our parents made us learn lines from Shakespeare by heart. That's why I've always been very good at Shakespeare.

"Once, when I was twelve, I wrote obscene graffiti on the wall of my father's chauffeur's lavatory. I was made to learn lines from *Julius Caesar*.

"O, pardon me, thou bleeding
piece of earth,
That I am meek and gentle
with these butchers.
Thou art the ruin …"

"Unfortunately for my parents, I found these lines attractive. That's why I had very little trouble learning them.

"I was made to learn lines from *Hamlet* as well, but I don't like that play. Sometimes, my mother lay on a sofa in front of an anglepoise lamp, muttering the words, "God, Hamlet was such a maddening young man!""

Ted giggled hysterically.

"What was the nature of the obscene graffiti which you wrote on the wall of your father's chauffeur's lavatory?" he asked

"I've forgotten. You seem such a sad, mysterious person, and yet you've got the most beautiful big brown eyes, I've ever seen. Not only that, your cock is nearly always swollen and you're so shy all the time. I also love the way your tie is permanently loosened at the neck, with the top two buttons of your shirt undone. This turns me on more than I can say in words." Natalie paused, "I can tell that you're a very unhappy person and that you're unhappily married as well. I've always been attracted to very sad men. May I go next door and play for you?" Ted smiled.

"Why, yes, Natalie. I don't mind," he said, adding, "you'd make a bloody good psychiatrist."

Natalie went into the next-door room, and she lifted the lid of the grand piano in there. She played *Für Elise*, *The Moonlight Sonata* and Handel's *Sarabande in D Minor*.

Ted came into the room, and laid his hands on her shoulders. He wished with all his heart, that he could seduce her, without being struck off by the GMC.

"That was so lovely, Natalie. You play beautifully. Where did you learn to play like that?"

"At school, mainly." Her reply was a trifle abrupt. She made a temporary decision to play "white" in this particular game of chess.

They lay on the floor in the piano room, on their backs. The carpet was threadbare and uncomfortable. Ted quickly became swollen. He pushed up her leopard-skin shirt and fondled her breasts. He was relieved by the fact that she wasn't wearing a bra.

He rubbed her clitoris vigorously until she screamed with joy. He unzipped his flies, brought out his cock and entered her body, gently at first, and gradually became more vigorous. She continued to scream, and gripped him tightly by the waist, which felt soft and moist, like the coat of a dog, which had just been taken for a run.

During the act, he screamed loudly in her ear. She feared for a moment that he was about to perforate her eardrum. She sat up and rested her arms on the carpet.

"Do you love me?" she asked foolishly. Marigold had once advised her never to ask a man a question of that nature. She regretted having done so.

"Don't fish, Nat," he replied obscurely.

Rex Malone had once said the same thing, but in

different circumstances. She had said nothing in return to either of the men.

There was a long silence. Natalie suspected that Ted was hiding something from her, but try as she did, she was unable to work out what it was.

"Although you seem very sad, most of the time, you appear quite carefree, at other times, but I can still tell that there was some event or other during your childhood which traumatised you beyond belief. Please tell me what it was. I would do anything to be able to understand you completely."

"My favourite brother was killed in a car crash when I was a boy," began Ted. It seemed that he was reluctant to tell Natalie something of such a personal nature.

"I'm so terribly sorry, Ted. How old were you at the time?"

"I was thirteen and my brother fifteen."

Natalie laid her hands on his.

"I'm sure you've never really got over that. Were your parents alive?"

"No, but I've completely got over the trauma of my brother's death now."

"It's still a dreadful thing for you to have had to bear, Ted."

"There was something else in my childhood, which was far, far worse. I was six at the time and I've never forgotten it."

"What was it, Ted? I hate asking you a question of this nature, but I feel it's the only way you can get it off your chest. Were you sexually assaulted by someone when you were six?"

"No!"

"Was it anything to do with your father?"

"No! No! No!" shouted Ted, adding, "my father was a clergyman."

"Please, please, tell me."

Ted was almost in tears.

"It was something to do with a nanny," he bleated eventually.

"A nanny? A nanny? What do you mean, Ted?" asked Natalie, adding,

"Did you have a nanny whom you loved very much, but who died when you were a child, and whose death broke your heart?"

"No. It wasn't anything like that, Natalie." There was another silence which was broken by Ted.

"My mother hired this nanny. My brothers were at school. I didn't have any sisters."

"What about the nanny, Ted?"

"She was Dutch."

"So what, if I might ask?"

"She had this unwholesome preoccupation with eggs. It didn't matter whether they were scrambled, fried, poached, boiled or whatever…"

"Eggs? What the hell are you talking about, Ted?" asked Natalie impatiently.

"The Dutch nanny persecuted me and tortured me. Ever since she tortured me, I have never been able to eat an egg of any kind in my life, or look at one either."

"Come on, Ted! What the hell are you talking about? What is all this business about eggs?"

"You don't realise how cruel she was, and I was only six! The nursery was a long way away from the dining room where my parents had breakfast. The nanny tied me to a chair, cut open an egg, and thrust it into my mouth, including the shells. In fact, the shells were even more horrible than the eggs themselves. I was sick every time and she made me eat the vomit."

"Why the hell didn't you tell your mother that this woman was doing this? Why couldn't your mother have given this woman an appropriate and detailed interview before she employed her? I don't understand why she didn't ask for a battery of references first.

"Incidentally, I take it you told your mother?"

"I don't know."

"What the fucking hell do you mean, you don't know? What about your father? Did you tell him?"

"No."

"Stop holding things back, Ted. I'm desperately trying to understand you and you're not helping me to do so. You're making me really angry. I've got every right to know. Why are you so weak?"

The following Tuesday, Natalie came into Ted's consulting room, with an egg in the palm of her hand. She didn't mean to hurt him. She only meant to tease him.

Ted's reaction shocked her terribly. It reminded her of her father's fainting attack in the south of France. Ted rushed to the sink in a cubby hole in a corner of his consulting room and was sick. When he returned to his desk, his complexion turned from green to white.

Natalie was ashamed and walked towards him. At the time, she had no idea how much she had upset him.

"I'm sorry, Ted," she ventured. "I only meant it as a joke. I didn't mean to hurt you."

He failed to accept her apology, because of the extreme gravity of his childhood experience.

"How would you like it if someone sent you a message, saying I was dying? I don't think you would like it at all, would you?"

"I did say I was sorry! Don't you think you are taking yourself far too seriously?" asked Natalie.

Natalie stayed in his room throughout the consultation time, however, and tried to humour him by playing the piano in the room next door.

Eventually, she returned to her flat, with her head lowered all the way there. She brooded for an hour or two. Finally, she phoned an old school friend to whom she was very close. Her name was Lyndsay. She was unusually pretty and had a shock of red hair.

Natalie was bright at school and did Lyndsay's French and Latin preps for her. In return, Lyndsay introduced her friend to men. Also, Lyndsay was street-wise and knew how to deal with them.

"How do you think I should deal with a man whom I have hurt?" asked Natalie.

"In what way did you hurt him?"

"It's impossible to explain. The man in question has a phobia about eggs."

"What do you mean, eggs?"

"I just don't understand. I didn't mean to upset him."

"Let me give you a word of advice," began Lyndsay. "If you really want to please a man, any man, make a point of cross examining him about his car."

"The man I go out with doesn't possess a car," said Natalie.

"That's strange," said Lyndsay. There was a long silence, broken by Natalie.

"Why do men like to be cross examined about their cars, anyway?" she asked eventually.

"I simply don't know. Maybe, it's because they are turned on by women, who do so. There's no other explanation that I know of, other than the fact that a lot of men love anything mechanical."

"Men are such strange creatures," said Natalie. "They are completely incomprehensible and at the same time so kind-hearted and gentle. They are also much weaker than women and have to be controlled, as opposed to the other way round. Another thing about them is that they are rarely scheming in anyway."

Natalie finally told Lyndsay the entire and bizarre truth about the egg.

"My friend's a psychiatrist," she added forcefully.

"Is he your psychiatrist?" asked Lindsey.

"Yes, he is."

"That's unusual. Mind you, you're pretty mad, yourself."

"If no one was mad, psychiatrists wouldn't be able to earn their living, would they?"

Once Natalie and Lyndsay had finished their conversation, Natalie wrote Ted a sweet letter in which she said she had absolutely no idea how much the egg incident had upset him, and added that she had been crying for hours because of her guilt. She begged him to forgive her.

***

She had employed an Irish maid called May, who suffered from dementia. Provided she took the appropriate pills every morning, she was able to suppress the symptoms of the disease, and appeared normal. Natalie liked her very much and she was good at domestic duties. She hoped May would stay in her employ as long as possible, provided she continued to take her pills.

May slept in a bedroom which contained two beds, and which faced the living-room. She occupied one bed and the other was empty.

There was a third room, formerly a bedroom, which Natalie used to keep her clothes in. She thought this room was haunted, as she had used it to take her overdose in, after Charlie's funeral. She slept on a bed in the living-room, instead. Natalie found this room comfortable, and it had a splendid view of the Thames.

She reminded May to take her pills every morning. She also told her to make the spare bed in her room on Tuesdays, because she had asked Ted to visit her in her flat on Tuesdays. She preferred May's room to his Harley Street consulting room.

"You do know how to make a bed, don't you?" she asked May.

"Oh, aye."

"Another thing, May, I know I may have told you about this matter before. A gentleman will be coming here at five o'clock and will be doing so every Tuesday. He will be leaving the flat at eight o'clock, afterwards," Natalie continued, as if she were speaking to a foreigner.

"This gentleman will need access to the spare bed in your room, every Tuesday, at five o clock, as I said. Do you understand my instructions?"

"Aye."

***

Ted turned up at Natalie's flat the following Tuesday. He had his own key to the flat, and Natalie waited for him, lying on her back in the spare bed, in May's room, while he went to the bathroom first.

May lay down in her own bed, however, and pulled the covers over her face, as if intending to go to sleep. She failed to notice her naked boss, lying in the other bed, waiting for her lover.

Ted went back to the bathroom and shaved. After a few minutes, he rushed into the spare bedroom and threw himself on top of Natalie's body, failing to notice May who was under the covers in the other bed. Natalie was enthralled by Ted's warm, heavy weight and the sweat accompanying it. The lovers screamed the building down, as they were about to come.

Natalie looked upwards at Ted's beautiful face, which was even more radiant, because of his sad, brown eyes and his lovely silvery hair. She gripped him tightly round the waist.

Suddenly, she saw May's mad, cadaverous face and staring eyes, barely an inch away from hers. Her face was just behind Ted's head. The whites of her eyes were shining, like those of a demented banshee.

The fact that May had not bathed for quite some time, caused Ted to suspect that the stench was coming from his mistress, rather than her servant.

"What the fucking hell do you think you're doing, May?" shouted Natalie.

"I've lost my radio, blast it! Where the hell is it?" asked May, in an anxious tone of voice, adding, "*The Archers* are on at seven o'clock, and I don't want to miss them."

May hit Ted on the back, with a gruesome paperback book penned by her boss, the first thing she could find, which was lying on the floor.

"Come on, sir! Where's my radio? Could you please stop whatever it is that you are doing, and find it?"

She sounded hysterical, like a sergeant major, addressing an inappropriately dressed private, late for parade.

"Indeed, I most certainly will not!" said Ted, his voice raised. His cock had gone limp inside Natalie, who burst into tears.

May's appearance terrified him. In his eyes, she looked like a disfigured gargoyle. He dressed as quickly as he could, rushed out of the room, and the flat, putting as much distance between himself and May as possible.

Natalie continued to cry. Even more unbelievably, May had got back into bed, pulled up the covers, as if she meant to go to sleep, and put the light out.

"Get out of that bed," said Natalie. "I'd like a word with you in the living-room." They sat down on one of the sofas.

"I want this behaviour changed," said Natalie mildly. She knew nothing about dementia at the time. She thought it might be a form of schizophrenia, which could be cured with medical aid.

"What were you doing?" asked May, who opened the conversation.

"I think it's fairly obvious what I was doing," said Natalie.

"You were lying on your back."

"Yes, of course, I was lying on my back. What did you think I was doing, lying on the bloody ceiling?"

There was a silence, which was broken by Natalie. "Do you know the Facts of Life, May?"

"No."

"I'll tell you then. Your mother must have told you about the Facts of Life when you were a child. Do you know, for instance, what your father did to your mother, in order to bring you into the world?"

"Not really."

"I find this very odd. I don't want to use ribald language, but I'm afraid I'm going to have to do so, and you are going to listen. Your father put his cock into your mother's cunt. In other words, he fucked her."

May was even more confused. She thought that her father had entered her mother's anus, to conceive a baby. She sniffed as if she were about to cry.

"Please don't use such disgusting language in front of me," she pleaded. She fiddled with her rosary beads, rose to her feet and returned to her bedroom. She knelt by her bed and prayed.

Despite the horrendous incident the night before, Natalie did not have the heart to sack May, mainly because her maid laughed at her jokes, and appealed to her exhibitionism.

Father's Walking Stick

Natalie was woken two days later by Ted's secretary, Isabel Armitage, who had a cold, abrupt, tinny voice. Natalie had an appalling telephone manner, because of her pathological fear of bereavement. She had feared this ever since Charlie had died.

"Miss Natalie Klein?"

"Fucking hell, yes!"

There was a silence, broken by the caller.

"This is Isabel Armitage, Dr Curruthers's secretary. I'm afraid Dr Curruthers is unwell and has had to retire indefinitely."

"What's wrong with him?" shouted Natalie.

"This is all I'm prepared to say."

"Where can I get hold of him? Is he in hospital?"

"I can't tell you any more than I have told you already."

"Is he very seriously ill?" bellowed Natalie. (She realized she was even more in love with Ted, simply because he was out of her reach.)

"Well, he is, and he isn't," replied Isabel, her voice devoid of emotion, once more.

"Either he is, or he isn't!"

"There is very little I can add," repeated Isabel coldly.

Natalie burst into tears.

"No bastard reduces Natalie Klein to tears, without getting their comeuppance. I am a B.A. Hons graduate, and I am also a distinguished woman of letters, with over twenty-five published books behind me. Two of these have been translated into Russian. Some are even read by Russian children! You, on the other hand, are no more than a shorthand typist."

Isabel, who was not particularly spontaneous, couldn't think of anything further to say.

"Well, that's as may be," she commented eventually.

Natalie bombarded Isabel with a battery of abusive language. She uttered about ten sentences in all, teaching the secretary a cacophony of new words. Isabel hung up in disgust.

Natalie would not be broken. She took a black cab to 113 Harley Street, hoping to find someone there, who would be able to give her more helpful information about Ted's condition. She arrived and rang the bell. The door opened automatically, as always.

She saw an unknown woman behind the reception desk. The woman was shabbily dressed, her face and nails were unpainted, and her breath was foul. She was playing *Solitaire* on her computer.

"What the hell's wrong with Dr Curruthers?" asked Natalie aggressively.

The woman looked bored and shrugged her shoulders. She spoke with a thick, Italian accent.

"I know nothing," she said casually, and continued to play *Solitaire*.

Natalie's emotional pain was worse than it had ever been before, except when she had been told that her beloved Charlie had died. She completely lost it and had no idea what she was saying.

"I happen to be a close personal friend of the Prime Minister's, and as such, I have the authority to drop a hydrogen bomb on Rome. The fallout will spread all over Italy and will even reach Sicily. All your friends, family members and relatives will automatically be annihilated."

Natalie paused for breath. "However, if you co-operate with me, and tell me what's wrong with Dr Curruthers, and also where he is, no harm will come to you. If you do not cooperate, I will instruct my chauffeur to drive me to Whitehall, where I will press the appropriate buttons."

A British receptionist, with peroxide blonde hair, already known to Natalie, came downstairs and threatened to call the police. Doctors, dentists, and medical secretaries gathered on the staircase, hoping to witness an entertaining scene. Natalie turned to the British receptionist.

"If you don't tell me what is wrong with Dr Curruthers, or where he is, I'll go straight to your house, and I'll seduce your husband!" she said. Natalie's words were uttered in vain because the receptionist was a lesbian.

"Dr Curruthers has retired from medical practice altogether, because of ill health. Kindly leave or I'll have to call the police."

"What the hell's wrong with him? I've got every right to know," said Natalie, adding, "Maybe you don't realise this.

I'm hopelessly in love with him. Aren't you a woman yourself? Have you never loved a man? I'm not made of iron."

Her moving words had no effect on the receptionist, however.

"The police are on their way," she said coldly.

Natalie was even more enraged, and decided to show the receptionist the most extreme form of exhibitionism that she could muster.

"You have no idea how wretched I am. There are no electric vibrators in the shops. I'm even having to use one of my father's walking sticks!"

"You are disgusting! Hopefully you will be put in a cell."

Within about ten minutes, a single policeman, accompanied by a menacing-looking Alsatian dog, stormed onto the premises.

"Miss Natalie Klein?"

"Yes."

"What seems to be the trouble? I understand you was threatening to drop a hydrogen bomb on Rome. You're a brick short of a load," said the policeman mildly.

"Fucking bloody Bollocks! I never threatened to drop a hydrogen bomb anywhere. I'm upset because one of my psychiatrists has gone missing!"

"Oy? 'Ow many 'ave you got?"

"I'm a BA Hons. university graduate and a distinguished woman of letters. I have written at least twenty-five books," said Natalie.

"I'm not interested in the number of books you've written," said the policeman. He tightened the Alsatian's lead. The dog frothed at the mouth.

"If that dog bites me, I'll have it put down!" said Natalie.

"You've caused a major disturbance in a doctor's surgery, as well as a breach of the peace, and have used obscene language as well, so I'm slinging you down the nick," said the policeman. He radioed to his driver in the panda car outside.

"I'm far too important to be slung down nicks!"

Natalie was handcuffed by the policeman, and ushered into the back of the panda car. His colleague was behind the wheel.

"You've caused a breach of the peace, as my colleague has just informed me, and in doing so, you've broken the law," said the driver.

"If nobody ever broke the law, the police wouldn't be able to earn a living, would they?" said Natalie. Her joke was ignored.

She was taken to the nearest police station. There were not enough cells, so she was left standing near the desk sergeant. Neither Natalie, nor the desk sergeant spoke for at least ten minutes.

"I'll have you know that I keep a bust of Sir Winston Churchill in my flat," said Natalie, adding, "My maid, who's a bit gaga, accidentally dropped a soiled handkerchief on top of it, but I was far too kind to sack her. Most employers would have done so."

The sergeant was hardly a Wildean conversationalist.

"Did she, now?" he eventually managed to mutter.

After an hour or two, Natalie was told she could go home. She rang Isabel, the following day in tears, yet again. She hadn't been able to sleep and couldn't eat either.

***

The love-sick newspaper baron's daughter made a hair appointment, having realized that she looked a mess. She was known to two separate hairdressers, who despised each other because they poached each other's clients. One was a surly Indian called Rajiv Patel. The other was good company and was always joking. He was an Irishman called Johnny Ryan.

"You'd cause trouble in an empty house, you would!" he said sometimes, when he was doing Natalie's hair. This remark invariably made Natalie laugh.

Whenever she gave a book launch, she invited the two hairdressers together, so that they would get into a fight, and hopefully win Natalie more publicity. Patel referred to Johnny as "Pitbull" and Johnny referred to Patel as "the cunt". Only Patel was available on that sad day. His salon was almost full. Natalie sat down, burst into floods of tears, and sniffed continuously.

"I do wish you'd stop that bloody sniffing!" said another client, a woman of about Natalie's age.

"I'm terribly upset, O.K.? I've just received some very distressing news!" shouted Natalie. The other client was disinterested. She ignored Natalie and told everyone in the salon, what a wonderful skier she was. She had a loud, resonant voice, and her words reverberated down the corridor outside the salon. Her voice was not unlike Natalie's.

"I hope you fall down a bloody crevasse!" shouted Natalie.

Patel was embarrassed by his erring clients, but he was too cowardly to take sides.

"What do you want done, Natalie?" he asked. Natalie had a sudden urge to shock the people around her, the majority of whom were quite elderly, in their seventies and eighties, unlike the woman who had boasted of her skiing prowess.

"All I want to do is suck his fucking cock!" shouted Natalie.

Patel had been working on an eighty-year-old lady's hair. He dropped his comb and jumped backwards in disgust.

"I will not tolerate disgusting language in here. I'd like you to leave," he said.

"I'll leave with pleasure. Incidentally, Johnny Ryan does my hair much better than you do. I only came here this afternoon because I couldn't get a booking in his salon earlier.

"He also says that you persuade old ladies, to make you beneficiaries of their wills. It's not only he who says that. You've got a reputation for behaving in this way, all over London!"

The scissors fell from Patel's hands, and his eyes widened like saucers. "This is slander!" he shouted. "Don't ever come back to my salon again."

"Don't you remember fitting diamond tiaras onto my mother's hair, when you were about sixteen, before the Opening of Parliament each year? Your connection with my family goes back for years. I couldn't bear seeing you making a fool of yourself," said Natalie. Her voice was raised to such an extent, that all Patel's clients could hear her words.

She left, and thought of the future, when she would be able to tell Johnny Ryan about her dispute with Patel.

It was raining hard. On her way home, Natalie felt very depressed. As she would not have been able to have her hair done at Patel's salon anymore, she stared at her reflection in few shop windows, and was pained by the appearance of her hair.

She hoped that Johnny would be able to do her hair the next day, and called him on her mobile. She was his favourite client, as she always gave him substantial tips. He said he could fit her in at two o'clock the following day.

She felt fractionally more optimistic and got drunk that evening. Instead of ringing Isabel Armitage the next morning, she surfed through the *Yellow Pages* and eventually found the name, Saul Cohen, Private Detective. Next to his name, was an exemplary reference.

Saul lived in Golders Green, a Jewish area. Natalie had always got on well with Jewish people, such as Rex Malone, Festenstein and many others, all of whom she numbered among her closest friends. She got on well with them because she regarded them as being warm, hard-working, loyal and above all, kind. Although there were exceptions to this rule, these were few and far between.

Natalie left a message on Saul's mobile, and asked him where and when it would be convenient for the two to meet. Her action of surfing *Yellow Pages* was a superb alternative to ringing Ted's secretary, who invariably reduced her to tears.

Saul returned her call within half an hour, and suggested that they meet in a pub called *The Constitution* in Westminster at eight o'clock that evening. They sat alone in a corner of the pub. Natalie drank several gin and tonics and Saul had a pint of *Director's* beer. Natalie had seen Johnny Ryan earlier, and was satisfied by the way he had done her hair.

She gave Saul a detailed description of Ted's appearance, as well as his full name. She also provided two photographs of him, both of which were attractive. She told Saul that Ted lived in Hampstead.

Saul opened his briefcase, on which the initials S.C. had been engraved in gold letters. He produced a camera, several maps, a computer and a pair of binoculars. Natalie was impressed by the contents of his briefcase and his time-keeping. She was also attracted by his casual clothes and his bright, green eyes.

"My fee for tracking down missing adults is two thousand pounds," said Saul. He sounded business-like and Natalie liked his Star of David, which he wore on a chain round his neck. Although he was a complete stranger to her, she forced herself to trust him. After all, if she couldn't trust him, she wouldn't have been able to trust anyone, for that matter.

"That sum's very generous," she said. "I always thought private dicks charged twice as much as that."

Saul smiled. He had a central gold tooth in his top jaw.

"Oh, you did, did you? If that were the case, very few people would be able to afford private dicks. You gave me your home address and mobile number, on the message you left for me. I know a decent Italian restaurant called the *Solo Mio Uno*, in Belgrave Road, near where you told me you lived. When we get to the restaurant, we'll exchange contracts. There'll be a copy for yourself and a copy for me," Saul added, "I suggest we meet at the Italian at about seven o'clock, in about a week's time. Wednesdays always suit me best.

Natalie suddenly noticed that Saul spoke with a slightly Yiddish accent, combined with a Bronx accent. She found his brogue attractive.

He continued, "I will need at least five days to complete my research, not to mention my use of the Internet. I've got a computer, which I think you saw."

***

They sat down at a table, covered by a white cloth. Natalie took her cheque book from her bag and wrote Saul a cheque for two thousand pounds.

"I've never understood the Internet," she confessed. "I use a pen and paper to write my books with. What sort of information does the Internet provide you with?"

"You'd be surprised how miraculously the Internet works. It will confirm the exact whereabouts of your friend's house in Hampstead, and will even reproduce photographs of the exterior and interior of the house including every room, as well as the garden. It will also print pictures of the street, in which his house can be found."

Saul produced a contract in duplicate, which he and Natalie signed on both sides. He did not hesitate to give her a receipt.

They had three courses and it was Natalie who paid the bill, because she thought it would seem proper, taking Saul's persistent kindness and reliability into account.

***

Saul rang Natalie, within about a week's time, once he had found out more about Ted's whereabouts. The detective was certainly a man of his word.

"I've found more about Ted, as requested," he began.

"First, I've discovered his address in Hampstead, although he is no longer living there, and the house is for sale at the moment.

"I spoke to a cleaner working in the house, though. She told me that Ted's marriage had broken down and that he had been admitted to a mental hospital in Scotland. She was adamant that Ted's whereabouts in Scotland should not in any way be disclosed to his wife. Her name is Belladonna. Jesus! What sort of a name is that?" Saul continued.

"Ted has apparently moved out of his house in Hampstead to be as far away from Belladonna as possible. I have managed to drive to Scotland in my BMW. I've studied one map after another, including the Internet of course. It was a hell of a trek. Thank God I've got a degree in Geography!

"The cleaner and I had a long conversation. She told me that Ted was incarcerated in a clinic called the *Bonnie Prince Charlie* in Scotland, where most people go when they are suffering from problems with their nerves.

"She told me it's one of the best mental hospitals in Scotland. She even said one of her cousins had been there once, with good results."

"I'm very impressed by what you've told me so far," said Natalie. "I don't suppose you're anywhere near this place?"

"I'm about sixty-five miles south of the hospital. The roads are good. I can't say anymore, Nat. I'll keep in touch."

After her conversation with Saul, Natalie fell into a deep sleep, but he rang her again, and woke her up at about ten o'clock in the morning.

"Who the hell is it?" she asked. (Her telephone manner was atrocious, and always had been, since Charlie's death.)

"It's Saul."

"Where are you?"

"You won't believe it, Nat. I'm at *Bonnie Prince Charlie's*. Ted's cleaner gave me a photograph of him. I showed it to a receptionist at the hospital. I told her I was a visiting relative and that I wished to see him. She directed me to the lift. He's on the third floor. Room number 581. I'll ring you after I've seen him."

Natalie waited for her phone to ring.

"How is he?" she demanded hysterically.

"When I first went into his room, he didn't know who I was. I said I was a psychiatrist who was standing in for him, in his practice, in his absence. I was very friendly of course, and asked him how he was feeling. I'm afraid he told me he was really depressed and lonely."

"Oh, dear."

"Don't despair, Nat. I asked him casually whether the name Natalie Klein meant anything to him. Then I asked him whether she had been a patient of his. He sat up in bed with a jolt, and said he was desperate to have this woman's phone number. I gave it to him and he's going to ring you straight away. I told him you were in London."

"Thank you, so much, Saul," said Natalie. Her phone rang after that.

"You've been very eccentric, Natalie," began Ted.

"Come now!"

"I've been told that you've been attacking members of my staff in my Harley Street consulting rooms, and for some reason, best known to yourself, you threatened to drop a hydrogen bomb on Rome! Another receptionist said you were a brick short of a load.

"What you failed to realise was that this wretched woman is a rip roaring, raving lesbian! She said she would have given anything to grab you by the boobs."

"I didn't know that," Natalie giggled.

"Christ Natalie, what the hell did you say to her?"

"I said that if she didn't co-operate with me, and tell me where you were, I'd go straight to her house and seduce her husband!"

Ted let out a guffaw, which fuelled Natalie's exhibitionism.

"Natalie! You bad, bad girl!" said Ted.

"I'm afraid I've got something to say which isn't very pleasant. You have treated me appallingly, by disappearing like that, and failing to tell me where you'd gone.

"Unless you can prove you're not a complete cad, I want nothing further to do with you. You broke my heart."

"I'm so sorry! I'm afraid I've been a very naughty boy! My pills have run out, so I'll be coming back to London, say in about two weeks' time, and I'll come straight to your flat. I've got your address. We'll meet every Tuesday afternoon at five o'clock as before. Then I'll tell you the whole story about my disappearance, which, incidentally, was not my fault. It was the fault of my evil wife, Belladonna."

"Even so, you really do owe me an explanation and an apology, for the terrible pain you inflicted on me," continued Natalie coldly, adding, "you've caused me so much misery, and your odious secretary, Isabel Armitage, has been so vile to me. She made me cry several times. No-one reduces Natalie Klein to tears, without getting their comeuppance!"

"I could be very much to blame, as well, actually" said Ted meekly. "I've been through the tortures of the damned. My evil wife has made it impossible for me to earn a living, and has also made it impossible for me to keep my rooms in Harley Street."

"A likely tale! Try that again!" shouted Natalie.

"Please listen to me, Natalie. Belladonna, and her vicious sister, Livia, went to the offices of the G.M.C. (the General Medical Council), and told the authorities there that, because of an operation I once had on a valve leading to my heart, fifteen years ago, it would never be safe for me to practice as a psychiatrist again. This is rubbish, but where the G.M.C. are concerned, once they've got you down the barrel of a gun, there's nothing you can do to fight them back.

"Also, I've suffered from other problems with the G.M.C. My wife told them that my heart operation had caused me to have minor problems with my brain. I have had God knows how many investigations, and there is nothing wrong with my brain."

"Is this really true?"

"Yes."

"How could anyone do such things to another human being?" asked Natalie in disgust.

"I'll tell you more about it, when I see you in London. I'm going to get some rest now. Incidentally, how on earth did you find that bloody private dick?"

"When I really want something, I go out of my way to get it. That's what Rex Malone taught me to do when I was little."

"Who's he?" asked Ted.

"I'll tell you one day," said Natalie.

***

Ted turned up, at Natalie's flat in London, at five o'clock, as arranged.

She fondled him in the private parts and licked his hands. "Welcome back, my beauty! I want to hear what really happened to you."

She made him some Yorkshire tea (his and her favourite). "You really are a brick, Natalie!" he said.

"Don't ever say that, Ted. That's exactly what Charlie said, just before he died."

Natalie continued to psychoanalyse her lover, as she had during their previous meetings, before his mysterious departure.

She sat next to him, on one of the sofas, and tried to unzip his flies. His zip was as stiff as it had been, when she had first met him in the lift in Harley Street.

"How's the whore?" she asked, as she continued to try to unzip him.

"Vindictive as ever," he replied.

She tried to undo his zip once more, but failed. "Please get it out, Ted! I think I'll go mad if you don't."

He squeezed his legs together.

"No, no, Ted! How can you be so cruel? I'm not made of iron!"

Ted suddenly felt guilty. He undid his zip, and pulled out his cock.

"Would you like me to have her duffed?" she asked. She rubbed part of his cock at the top, in the way he particularly liked, and licked it with the tip of her tongue. It didn't take him long to get hard.

"I like men who are circumcised," she said.

"What do you mean?"

"Don't you know? I like my lovers to be snipped. I always have."

He changed the subject, and referred to his wife.

"Revenge is a dish best served cold," he said obscurely.

"Bollocks! If Sir Winston Churchill had adopted that ridiculous attitude, the Germans would have won the war!" said Natalie, her voice raised.

"Belladonna is the mother of my children," said Ted, confrontationally.

"I don't give a fuck whose bloody mother she is! A woman called Klara Hitler was Hitler's mother, too. So what?"

There was a long silence, which was broken by Ted.

"I've got to earn my living, but Belladonna is preventing me from doing so, out of spite alone. She's trying to make me homeless, and to live on the streets of London."

He continued, his eyes watery, "At the moment, I have to 'sofa-surf' and live out of a suitcase. Sometimes, I have had no choice but to eat out of dustbins, and at other times, to try my luck at empty food-banks."

"Why can't you live here, Ted?" asked Natalie.

"Because you've still got that spooky maid in your flat."

May, Natalie's maid, who suffered from worsening dementia, continued to terrify Ted. Sometimes, she was asymptomatic, provided she took her pills each morning. Other times, she was frightening beyond belief.

Natalie thought briefly about Belladonna, and wondered how another woman could be so cruel to a man who had worked like a pit pony, mainly in her interests, all his life, to enable her to buy pretty clothes, shoes and to have her hair done, as well as a myriad of other things.

"Not once has she expressed a word of gratitude for my hard work, from one month to the next," said Ted.

"Please, Ted, tell me how I can help you. Although you've been disgracefully maligned, and robbed by that stinking prostitute, I've got plenty of money of my own, because I really enjoy writing my books. Also, my father's a wealthy press baron, and I've made quite a lot of money on my own steam. I can and will help you to lead a reasonably happy life."

She continued, "I've been brought up to be kind to those who have fallen on hard times. My father certainly wouldn't allow a hard-working man, like yourself, to be continuously robbed by a cheap vindictive tart." Ted stared into space and listened to Natalie's words.

"I'm not suggesting that you become a rent-boy, but if you were forced to live on the streets, it would really break my heart, more than I can say in words."

"I'm too proud to be a male prostitute, Natalie," said Ted.

"I wasn't suggesting that you become one."

He added, "can you consider giving me a reasonably handsome sum of money? It may not make a huge difference to you, but it would to me. I really am a broken man. Not only that, I've fallen in love with your mind."

"That's mighty civil of you," said Natalie. "When you're in trouble, I will pay your phone bills, and anything else you need within reason. I lay a particular emphasis on the words, "within reason". That way, I don't want to hear any more boring talk about male prostitution," she added, her voice raised.

There was a silence.

"In any relationship, there must be a tough and a weak party. You are beautiful beyond belief and my eyes need you. I am strong, whereas you are weak, because of the fact that your father was a clergyman, maybe. Also, you appear only to be happy when that Belladonna bitch walks over you in stiletto heels."

Natalie spoke, yet again, this time at considerable length. She was running away with her own words.

"I have always preferred weaker men. That way, I have complete control over them. I am able to teach them the difference between right and wrong, and good and evil. Women are, on the whole, stronger, and more cossetted, than men, and nearly always have been. Men need to be protected despite the things that have been said in the past."

"You certainly do bang on, don't you, Nat?" said Ted mildly.

Despite her apparent lack of fear of anyone or anything, Natalie was afraid of asking Ted whether he was actually in love with her, as a person, or whether he was just in love with her mind.

There were some other minor things which troubled her, however, namely old age, rejection, loneliness and the dark, the last being due to her heinous memory of seeing Charlie's body in a mortuary, horribly presented.

There were times when Ted wished to spend more time in Natalie's flat, despite the presence of her mad maid, although sometimes he had a craving for space. However, on one Tuesday afternoon, they had been sitting on one of the sofas, and Natalie had become over-excited, and pulled him to the floor, on top of her. They had violent, noisy sex, but Ted was rather clumsy and inadvertently kicked over the urn, containing Charlie's ashes. Natalie didn't say anything, because she was afraid of upsetting him.

"You're to kill that stinking tart!" she shouted after the sex act had ended. "If you don't kill her, I will."

He wondered for a fleeting moment, as confused men sometimes do, whether Natalie's love for Charlie, had been greater than her love for him. After all, he recalled that she had taken an overdose on the morning after Charlie's funeral, indicating that she no longer wished to live.

"Do you ever think about Charlie these days?" asked Ted, with a touch of jealousy, as well as curiosity, in his voice. They were sitting on the sofa once more.

"Yes, I think about him every night, before I go to sleep. That is when you're not here. Sometimes, I cry. My grief is so intense that I can never sleep with the light off. When he was dead, he was in such a dreadful state, that I beat the mortuary attendant with my walking stick.

"I still have the most horrible nightmare which is recurrent. This is brought on whenever I am in the dark. As he is being pulled out of the drawer, he is actually alive and sobbing. When I look at him, I see maggots crawling out of his stomach."

Natalie continued, unable to stop her words.

"There was another thing which moved me very much. Charlie and I were watching a Holocaust film on the television once.

"Vanessa Redgrave was the main character in the film and her head had been completely shaved. So were the heads of all the other characters.

"Charlie was deeply upset, and wept piteously.

"I'm trying to be a gentleman," he said, quite out of the blue. That really distressed me, and I had to turn the film off.

"There was another occasion when he was terribly upset. I made him cry, when I was very drunk, in Marseille. I had no idea what I had said. He looked so beautiful when he was crying. He said, "I'm only a little man. If I didn't love you as much as I do, I'd want you out of my life. You're a nasty woman.""

"I was so guilty and ashamed, that I cried for two nights. I had no idea exactly what I had said, though. The incident still haunts me, particularly when I am alone."

Natalie began to sob convulsively. She continued, "There were two things Charlie used to say. One was, "Never make an enemy if you can possibly make a friend." The other was, "It costs nothing to show consideration towards another human being." When he was still in hospital, but feeling a bit better, he danced in front of the children on the paediatric ward to amuse them. He also made a point of offering to shop for his next-door neighbours, and delivered cards at Christmas by hand." Natalie couldn't stop crying.

Ted ran his hands through her hair, although it had just been set. He couldn't bear to see her in such pain, and he was in tears as well.

"I'm so sorry, Nat! You're such a good girl, such a very, good girl. Only time will flush away your horrendous memories."

He added, "I had no idea that someone with a terribly powerful personality like yours, was capable of such suffering."

"It's gruesome and black thoughts which keep me alive, Ted. When I was little, I used to go to strangers' funerals. I got a kick out of watching the coffins being lowered into the graves. This is hereditary of course. I get it from my maternal grandmother who had a taste for morbid matters, and who attended the trial of Dr Crippen, when chopped up pieces of his murdered wife's body were being passed round the court. She attended other sensational court cases, even if it meant her having to queue for hours outside the courts.

"I invited my father's gardener's daughter to attend a funeral with me," continued Natalie. "Her name was Ruth. When the coffin was being lowered, I turned to her and said, "Oh, Ruth, isn't it wonderful?" All she could say in return was, "Isn't the story of the murders of the Princes in the Tower, sad?""

***

Natalie made an appointment to see Dr Festenstein, to ask him whether Ted's problems were really as terrible as he made them out to be. The swarthy, Leipzig doctor told her that Belladonna planned to forbid her husband to walk his daughter down the aisle at her wedding, in three weeks' time. He also told her that she meant to lock him out of their unsold house in Hampstead for as long as possible.

Natalie warned her lover that Belladonna intended to lock him out of the house. Natalie drove her Ford Focus to a leafy area near the house, where Ted had been trying to kick the front door down. It was nine o'clock in the evening and she rang her lover on her mobile, to warn him, that his wife was going to lock him out. It was the second time that she had made the call.

"You will break that fucking door down, Ted, or I will never speak to you again! Be a man!"

"A man can't serve two masters," Ted called out.

"Yes, he can! It is I whom you will serve, not her."

Natalie was overtly aware of the close friendship between Festenstein and Ted, and of the fact that Festenstein took his friend out to lunch once a week, knowing that he had often gone without food, for days on end.

"My daughter's in the house, as well as my wife. I don't want to upset her," said Ted.

"I don't care if Jack the Ripper's in the house. Break the bloody door down!"

"The door's made of steel. It's too thick. I can't possibly break it down, Natalie."

"Break one of the windows, then."

"There'd be glass all over the floor," replied Ted.

The situation was unresolved. Ted spent the night in a damp, bed and breakfast nearby, and left early in the morning, without being able to pay the bill. All his chances of earning a living, without stealing, had been taken away from him once more. He wandered aimlessly round the streets of London. He had nothing to eat, that day, except a packet of crisps, which he had taken from a dustbin. He was far more than a broken man. He began to think about suicide and even confessed his wish to Festenstein. He also rang Natalie, and told her what he planned to do. She sobbed for about three days and finally rang the Samaritans. Unfortunately, she spoke to the same man, she had spoken to on another occasion, when she had rung the organisation and demanded that he visit her flat to change a typewriter ribbon at four o'clock in the morning!

***

During the period when he had not only worked hard, but had greatly enjoyed his work, relieving unfortunates of their misery, Ted had always been gregarious at the close of day, and gone to pubs with his friends and colleagues, of whom he had many. He had been well off then, and regularly paid for rounds, as well as giving money to beggars on pavements. He fervently believed in helping those who were less fortunate than he.

He was content at that time, and his most pleasant experience was visiting his children's twin bedroom, after dinner, and reading to them, until they fell asleep.

Natalie was determined to enable Ted to walk his daughter down the aisle at her wedding. She was fortunate indeed, in that Saul had a partner, who manned his office in Golders Green during his absence. Saul had gone to the Holy Land for about three weeks, to visit his relatives.

His partner's name was Moses who was very obliging. He had access to Natalie's files and was able to give her all the names of Ted's family members. His daughter's name was Cindy. She was melancholic like her father, and was seventeen.

She had an elder brother, called Eddie. There were no other children. The church, St Joseph's, was close to the house which Ted and Belladonna had been living in.

Natalie took a mini cab to the church, on Saul's partner's instructions. Ted had been there before.

Cindy was sitting on a flight of steps outside the church. Although her wedding dress flattered her figure, there were tears in her eyes. Natalie sat near her, but neither recognised the other.

Cindy was due to marry an American, five years older than she, called Wilbur Hazlett, who hailed from the Bronx district in New York. She failed to look at him, while he was getting out of the marital car, and wasn't particularly enamoured by his appearance. In fact, she found him repellent.

He was wearing a vulgar, pink-sequinned suit, and his black hair was Brylcreemed. He sported greasy, out-of-date sideburns, and his complexion was poor.

Cindy had told most of her friends in London, that she only intended to marry this beatnik, to get away from her evil mother. Curruthers was neatly and conventionally dressed in tails. It was possible that his smart outfit had been hired from a second-hand shop.

He looked very sad, and advanced half-heartedly towards Cindy, who had begun to walk forwards in slow motion, as if she were having a bad dream. Wagner's *Bridal March* blasted through the church and cheered her up a little.

Belladonna used extremely persuasive language to try to force Cindy's brother, Eddie, to walk her down the aisle, instead of her father. Natalie had been to Harrods the day before, and found a smart outfit for the occasion. She wore a veil, and her hair was impeccably coiffed, which caused her to look like a young Parisian model. She had on a tight, pale orange suit, a patent black belt and matching black patent shoes. She walked forwards with a spring in her step and approached Ted.

Belladonna was sitting in the front row, accompanied by her equally vicious sister, Livia. Belladonna was poorly dressed, which suggested that hate, rather than vanity, had been her sole motive for bothering to turn up at all. She had short, rust-coloured hair and looked offensively nondescript.

Natalie made a sudden, unexpected movement in Ted's direction, easing him towards Cindy, who tripped on one of the flagstones, falling over. The *Bridal March* came to an abrupt halt. Eddie hurriedly made his way to the place where his sister had fallen, to enable his father to do his duty.

Natalie helped Cindy to her feet, and gave her a radiant smile. She grabbed Ted by one of his arms, while Cindy stared at her father aghast. The girl looked almost triumphant. Her face was filled with hatred towards her mother, due to the older woman's unvarying cruelty towards her father. A few members of the congregation turned round and stared, on hearing the commotion.

Natalie seized Ted's other arm, and guided it towards that of his daughter. "Take her bloody arm, Ted! You're her father, aren't you? Where are your guts?"

Belladonna pushed other members of the congregation aside, and made her way towards the back of the church.

"Who the hell are you?" she asked Natalie, her voice raised.

"Never you mind who I am! I've come here to teach you the difference between good and evil. You'll see me again, in times less happy than these!"

Despite Ted's customary gentle mien, he was furious with Natalie, after everyone had left the church, to attend the reception. Also, Wilbur had become disillusioned by the eccentric behaviour of the British. He walked towards the marquee, where the reception was about to take place. When Cindy tentatively took his arm, for convention's sake, he pushed her roughly away, saying, "I'm quitting! I've had enough of you Brits. You're all weird!"

Although Wilbur had already written his speech, he tore up his notes and stamped on them, in a fit of rage, while Cindy gaped at him, with tears of embarrassment streaming down her cheeks.

Her tears were not due to her loss of Wilbur, but to the fact that she would have to stay with her mother somewhere, until another more eligible boyfriend presented himself.

Natalie and Ted walked down a narrow, leafy path, near the church. Ted broke the long silence between them.

"I bitterly disapproved of the way you interfered with my daughter's wedding," he said mildly.

"I had no choice but to do what I did, Ted. I had to show the wedding guests the difference between good and evil. I couldn't stand by and allow that bitch to destroy you, in a public place. Had I completely ignored what she was trying to do to you, I would have been crucifying myself, and you as well," said Natalie, forcefully.

She added, "You may not fully understand my motives at the moment, but you will in time. You are weak and I am strong, as I have said many times before. One day, you will come to understand the merits and courage of such women as Joan of Arc and Boudicca, as opposed to feeble characters, such as King Richard II of England and King Henry VI of England. King Henry VI was a fantastic flop. All he did was found bloody Eton.

"My function is to love, worship and protect you, Ted. It's time you realised my motives. That's the reason I do these things."

"How did you find your way to the church?" was all Ted could think of asking her, in a bemused tone of voice.

"I might have taken a black cab, mightn't I?" replied Natalie obscurely.

"Are you going to do anything like this again?" asked Ted. Part of him was terrified of Natalie. The other part adored and worshipped her.

"How can I possibly answer a question like that?" she replied. "If I see some bastard trampling over you, I will injure that person, because it would be my duty to do so.

"Besides, your daughter was far happier on your arm, than she could possibly have been on her brother's. I hail from a Welsh family, not a clergyman's family, in which children are brought up to turn the other cheek."

"You're much more like a man than a woman. Things should be the other way round," said Ted, spontaneously.

"I don't really see why things should be the other way round, not in these days, at any rate," replied Natalie. "We are living in 2021, not 1930. Don't you think that what you said just then, was rather chauvinistic?"

Ted said nothing. He knew Natalie was right, and that basically, he really was weaker than she, as she had pointed out to him.

The lovers went to a local pub, where they each had an alcoholic drink before changing into ordinary clothes in a back room. Ted wanted to drive, despite having had a drink. Natalie was exhausted and allowed him to take the wheel of her *Ford Focus*. They headed for the Embankment. He smoked throughout the journey.

"You look very sexy when you smoke," said Natalie. She stretched out her hand and stroked his thigh. It appeared that he had forgiven her for her reckless behaviour earlier that day, although he seemed very low in spirits.

"It's just as well that dreadful-looking American called off the wedding," he said eventually. "Can you imagine what kind of children that frightful man would have brought into the world? What if Cindy had had daughters? I can't stand American women's accents and speech modes, and the way they always swing their heads about, whenever they feel they're making a point."

Natalie laughed out loud.

"There's another thing I can't stand about Americans," added Ted. "It's the way they tend to fire guns out of their fucking cars!"

Natalie laughed again.

Ted pulled into the side of the road outside Natalie's flat, and had sex with her in the back of the *Ford Focus*. He didn't enjoy the sex act this time, because of his continuing low mood and endless embarrassment. A policewoman interrupted them after they had completed the sex act.

She spoke very quietly, and asked Ted whether or not he owned the car.

"What? I can't hear you?" said Ted.

"Do you own this car?" the policewoman asked once more.

"No. My friend does," he replied abruptly.

"Would you mind getting out of the vehicle, please?" said the policewoman.

Ted was unable to hear her whispering, inaudible voice.

"Do speak up! You're not talking to a fucking ant!" he shouted.

He was breathalysed, but only just passed the test. He was charged with the use of foul language towards a policewoman, and was asked to appear at a Magistrate's Court. The magistrate bumbled on and on about the need for him to attend anger management classes. The retired psychiatrist tried to imitate Natalie's mode of speech, for a fleeting moment.

"Oh, do shut up, and just tell me how much I owe you!"

When the amount was quoted, Ted pulled a dog-eared chequebook from his pocket. Most of the cheques were bouncers.

"All right. Who the hell do I make this out to?" he asked aggressively.

"You don't write out cheques in the dock. You write them in the front office!" said the magistrate.

"Where the hell's the front office?"

"I would like to remind you of your language once more."

Natalie was also in the courtroom and smiled broadly throughout the hearing. She took her lover out to a two-course lunch in the West End. She had three gin and tonics. He had a bottle of red wine. They went to bed in Natalie's flat and had unsatisfactory sex once more.

Ted still felt very low in spirits after the act. Natalie was bored and decided to take a break from her lover, the following morning. It wasn't long before she began to miss him sorely.

She invited herself to her sister's house. Marigold had moved and lived in a different house to Selwyn's. She told her sister that she needed to continue with her writing. So far, she had been so preoccupied with Ted, and his problems, that she had done very little work. Also, her publisher had requested the return of her manuscript within six weeks.

She soon regretted having gone to Marigold's house, because unbeknown to her, her sister had an unbelievably boring guest staying with her. He was a funeral director, called Douglas Crumblebottom, the former partner of Simon Bongwit.

Crumblebottom and Bongwit had been rivals of Natalie's and Charlie's, in the distant past, and Natalie was painfully reminded of her previous career, much of which had been happy.

The two undertakers had split up and gone their separate ways, because of a bitter quarrel over a woman. Strangely, they were in a pub when they had broken into a brawl. Crumblebottom had always struck Natalie as being a crashing bore with no sense of humour.

"This is my sister, Natalie Klein," said Marigold, as Natalie came through the front door.

"I remember you only too well, Miss Klein. You ruined one of my funerals," said Crumblebottom. "You instructed a pallbearer on your firm to paste a message on the windscreen of one of my hearses, saying, "AM DRUNK, WILL REMOVE VEHICLE WHEN SOBER."

"The message took an interminable amount of time to remove, and the funeral was delayed, for at least an hour and a half."

Natalie giggled.

"Natalie really!" exclaimed Marigold.

Crumblebottom was in his late fifties, and throughout his stay in Marigold's over-heated house, he wore a thick fur-lined overcoat, and smoked a foul-smelling pipe, without asking his hostess whether or not he could do so.

"I'd rather you didn't do that, because the tobacco from your pipe gets into the curtains, which means they will frequently have to be cleaned," said Marigold mildly.

Crumblebottom ignored his hostess and continued to smoke his pipe. Not only did he continue to indulge in this anti-social habit, he had pungent body odour. This was not the worst aspect of Crumblebottom's behaviour. He dominated the conversation at every meal, by speaking about the number of funerals he had officiated over, ever since about 1960, and occasionally, even earlier than that.

Whenever someone interrupted him, he ignored them and continued to speak about his subject, which his listeners found morbid, tedious and intensely depressing.

He received several lengthy mobile phone calls, while his companions were trying to make conversation. He also referred to cremations as "crems", which Natalie considered to be frightfully common.

He rose to his feet after coffee had been served, during his last evening at Marigold's, and expressed a wish to go to the "toilet".

"We don't use that word, where I come from," said Natalie, who felt she had come to the end of her tether, without Ted.

"There's no need to be rude, Natalie," said Marigold.

Natalie continued to yearn for Ted, his warm flesh, his incomparable physical beauty, his loud screams, and his lovely, brown eyes and silvery hair. Crumblebottom sipped noisily from a brimming glass of sherry, after each meal, particularly dinner. The fact that Natalie was in writers' block, as well as being away from her lover, caused her to be in a foul temper. She mimicked a coarse, Cockney accent, and said, "There ain't much business for you in this 'ouse, Guv."

"Natalie! How dare you be so fucking rude to Mr Crumblebottom!" shouted Marigold.

Crumblebottom cleared his throat loudly, hoiked up a lump of blood-drenched phlegm, and put an increased amount of tobacco into his pipe, generating an even more distasteful smell throughout the house, despite Marigold's having told him not to do so.

"Neither I, nor members of my staff, ever use that disgusting word in front of my customers," Crumblebottom stated forcefully.

Natalie had hysterical giggles, brought on by her troubled nerves. Ted had failed to ring her for several days. She was also irritated by Crumblebottom's crude behaviour and appalling manners. She fanned the air to minimise the disagreeable smell generated from his pipe.

"You'd better leave, Natalie," said Marigold. "I can't tolerate any more of your embarrassing behaviour."

The younger sister went upstairs, packed her suitcase and gathered her papers together. She didn't care about the offence she had caused to her sister, as she knew the two would be reconciled before long. She believed in the *cliché*; blood is stronger than water.

***

Natalie drove down the M40, and headed for her flat in the pouring rain. The weather conditions depressed her. She let herself into her flat and rang Ted several times, but to no avail. She wondered whether he had decided to walk out on her. She reasoned that that would have been unlikely, because of her continuous financial help towards him.

After all, she had paid all his phone bills, and his private doctor's bills when necessary. It crossed her mind that he might have been taken ill and had been admitted to hospital.

She thought briefly about her bombastic behaviour at Ted's daughter's wedding, although she knew that what she had done was right. She rang Ted several times each day, and left endless messages for him, but his silences continued. Sometimes, she relieved herself by going to the cinema to look at horror films. There were times when she watched macabre videos at home, over and over again.

Occasionally, she invited herself to other people's houses for dinner. She bored her hosts to tears, by speaking about Ted, and his physical beauty, but no one she spoke to, had heard of him, or knew what he looked like for that matter.

Ten days passed. Apart from the company of a few of her friends, she was alone and wretched. The only person who kept her company, sometimes, was her dotty maid, May, who laughed at her black-humoured jokes sometimes. May's mind, however, was deteriorating, and she perpetually set radiators on fire, by turning them upside down.

Natalie continued to wait. Finally, she phoned Ted's rival, Dr Isaac Stone at 113 Harley Street. It pained her to the core to have to sit in the ground floor waiting room, however, where she used to wait for Ted to collect her, in the past.

Stone was punctual. Natalie suddenly remembered what Ted used to say about his bizarre appearance.

"You are smiling, Miss Klein," he observed, once the two were in the lift, on their way to his consulting room. "Why are you smiling?"

"Oh, nothing."

"Indeed, it is something, rather than nothing. Incidentally, I will address you as Natalie, as opposed to "Miss Klein"."

Despite his initial attempt at familiarity, his overall manner was stiff and uninviting, just as it had been when he had seen her fellating his rival in the lift.

"Perhaps you would kindly tell me why you are smiling?" repeated Stone.

"Someone once said that your suits were so loud that they could be heard from Algeria. Also, that person commented that your car was in very poor condition."

"Oh, they did, did they? Was it that scoundrel, Curruthers, who passed these slanderous remarks?"

"I'm afraid I can't remember." Stone appeared to lose interest. The two got out of the lift. He unlocked the door leading to his huge consulting room. It was ostentatious, in that it had a heavy, gold handle, similar to handles leading to Medici churches in some Italian cities.

Unlike Curruthers' consulting room, Stone's was covered with elaborate gold artefacts, and gold-backed chairs. There was a gold, studded couch in a corner of the room, near a window, which overlooked Harley Street.

"Where do you wish to sit, Natalie?" asked Stone, his tone of voice still lacking in warmth.

"I'll lie on the couch, please." Her manner was equally as stiff as Stone's. "There is something I would like to talk to you about," she added.

"Oh, there is, is there?"

Natalie noticed that Stone spoke with a slight upper-class accent. It was not a genuine upper-class accent, but it was mimicked and had a mild Belfast lilt.

"What do you want to speak to me about?" he asked.

"Your room is far too hot," Natalie began. "It's almost as if everything were ninety degrees in the shade. Your radiator is fully turned on, and you haven't even got a fan in the room either," said Natalie angrily.

She added, "Dr Curruthers' room is reasonably cool, in comparison with yours, and so is his receptionist's area."

Stone was irritated by Natalie's interminable torrent of words, and interrupted her, his tone very abrupt and irritable as before.

"I am far more interested in the state of your mind, than in your opinions about the working conditions of my staff! Why are you here?" he added rudely.

Natalie giggled nervously and Stone deftly handed her some tissues, enclosed in a gold box, without smiling. He thought she was in tears.

"A trouble shared is a trouble halved," said Stone, as stiffly as before. He was unashamed of his use of practically the oldest cliché in the English language.

"I think it's time you told me why you're here," he repeated.

There was a short silence.

"I'm hopelessly in love with Dr Curruthers," she confessed. "I love him to very distraction and misery. He's disappeared. I want to know where the hell he is."

"Curruthers?" mused Stone, trying to hide the baffled tone in his voice. "Have you consummated your love for him yet?"

Natalie cleared her throat. Although she loved to use revolting language, because it turned her on to shock others, Stone's question jolted her. She blushed and paused for a few seconds. Then she reverted to the coarse language of the gutter.

"The first thing I did, once he was in my flat, was to get up his leg. That is apart from the incident in the lift, when I sucked his cock that day."

Stone fiddled with the gold signet ring on the index finger of his right hand, and leant forward in his chair.

"You got up his leg?" he exclaimed, and hurriedly recorded Natalie's words in her notes. She felt rather self-conscious at first, but within a matter of seconds, she let herself go, even though she was still finding Stone's manner awkward.

"Oh, yes, once I got up his leg, I asked him to get his cock out of his flies, and sucked it, just as I did in the lift that day. It was then that you said, "Dash it all, Curruthers, I feel this is letting down the street!"

"I had to laugh, and so did all the other doctors I told about the matter. I believe in having a stalwart stock of doctors knocking about the place. You were being so bloody pompous. It didn't take Dr Curruthers long to get hard. He is a gentleman, so he came into the palm of my hand, instead of down my throat. It was weeks later that he fucked me."

Stone rose to his feet, and walked up and down his consulting room, like an expectant father. He had gone to Eton, as had Curruthers, but he had never been exposed to such disgusting language as Natalie's in his life.

"You're not very feminine," he remarked, in an attempt to humiliate her. "You're more like a laddish, eighteen-year-old male. Does it excite you to use such revolting language?"

"Yes," replied Natalie. She had terrified him, but had no idea that she had done so.

Stone opened a tin of snuff and inhaled some of it. He felt fractionally more at ease afterwards.

"Your honesty is admirable, Natalie, although I'm bound to say I don't care for you as a person," Stone commented, his voice still sounding as stiff as a board. He added, "In ordinary circumstances, I would have thrown you out – that is to say – crossed you off my books, because I find permanently offensive language repugnant, not to mention, downright common."

"God, you're pompous!" said Natalie once more.

Stone continued, "However, because you are no doubt an extraordinary woman, who will probably see me on a regular basis, I feel I am faced with no choice, but to continue to see you, whether I like it or not.

"I formed the opinion that you were as common as mud, when I witnessed your lewd behaviour on meeting you in the lift for the first time," Stone continued.

"I hope to use you for many a psychiatric conference, though, and thus will be able to fill up my CV, more than amply."

This was not Stone's sole motive for keeping Natalie on his books. He wished to find out what it was about his rival, that was so attractive and fascinating where women were concerned. He intended to copy his style and technique between the sheets. Stone was thought that he might possibly be able to use Natalie, as a kind of Eliza Doolittle figure.

Like Dr Curruthers, he, too, was obsessed by sex, but he was also terrified of being struck off the G.M.C.'s books. So frightened was he, that he was even prepared to take his foul-mouthed patient, to a hotel, rather than to his Harley Street consulting rooms. Even the thought of accompanying her to a hotel in another country, crossed his mind.

"You will come to see me again, next week, won't you, Natalie?" asked Stone in his off-putting tone of voice.

"I might, but on the other hand, I might not."

He helped her to put on her jacket, and accompanied her down to the hall in the lift. She faced away from him, as the lift went down.

"If Ted still doesn't answer any of my calls, I might condescend to turn up at your consulting room," said Natalie curtly. "Remember, I love Ted more than I can say in words. Incidentally, are you circumcised?"

"I am a psychiatrist," replied Stone, implying that he had no wish to answer her question.

Natalie was very depressed once more and waited for a black cab. May had forgotten to take her pills that day. The hall porter was off sick, and May was the only person in the lobby. She was stark naked, and had been walking up and down in the lobby for several hours.

She opened the front door, went outside onto the pavement, and spoke at length to a parked *Mini*.

Natalie returned to the building at about the same time, and found her maid on the pavement. Her first reaction was of sadness, but she tried to turn the incident into a joke.

"Hullo, May. It doesn't matter about your having a conversation with a *Mini*, but you could at least have spoken to a *Rolls Royce* instead!" she stated forcefully.

The police arrived and the naked May was taken to stay with one of her daughters, who, incidentally, was vehemently against the idea of her mother continuing to work for Natalie.

May soon came to enjoy her daughter's company, but Natalie felt lonely. She kept her next appointment with Stone, but at first, he was irritated by her failure to arrive on time. He had a cancellation, however, and was able to fit her in. Even so, she still disliked him intensely because of his ridiculous pomposity.

As Natalie walked down the steps of 113 Harley Street, after her appointment with Stone, she was suddenly overjoyed by the sight of Ted. He was sitting on the pavement, leaning against the railings. He was wearing the same clothes that he usually wore.

She was in tears of joy. "Where the hell have you been all this time? Why didn't you answer my calls? Charlie would never have behaved like this towards me."

Ted paused to breathe.

"Before you kick me in the balls, I can explain what happened. I've been very ill and in hospital with pneumonia. I have not been in the same place as my mobile phone."

"What hospital were you in?"

"The Royal Brompton."

Natalie and her lover took a black cab to her flat. She unlocked the front door. She filled a bath with hot water for him. While he was soaking in bath essence, she rang the Brompton Hospital to find out whether Ted had been a patient there or not. She discovered that he had indeed been a patient at the Brompton.

He came into the bedroom, wearing the same clothes, that he had had on, when the two had met in the street.

"I'm afraid I don't feel well enough for fun and games tonight," he said.

"Fair enough. We'll watch television if you like," she replied. "May's out and I'm no cook. I'll do you a plate of toast and marmalade and Yorkshire tea."

The lovers lay side by side and held hands. Eventually, they fell asleep. Ted was the first to wake up in the morning.

"I want to ask you a question, Natalie."

"What is your question?"

"When we met in Harley Street, I saw you coming out of the building, which I had been sharing with Isaac Stone. That is, after I'd been to hospital."

"Yes, what about it?"

"What were you doing there?"

"I went there because I was feeling terribly depressed, through not knowing where the hell you were. Also, none of my friends were in London."

"I'm so sorry! I'd lost my phone. Incidentally, what did you think of bloody old Stone?"

"I think he's very attractive," lied Natalie.

"Are you trying to make me jealous?" asked Ted.

Natalie was silent for a short time.

"Did you go to bed with him?" her lover asked suspiciously.

"No. I only saw him as a patient."

"You saw me as a patient, too. As far as you're concerned, that doesn't appear to have made much difference, does it?"

"You're hitting me below the belt, Ted. You just fucked off, without even asking someone to ring me up, to tell me whether or not you were alright."

Ted changed the subject.

"Did you know Stone was suspended once for having sex with one of his patients?" he asked mischievously. "In fact, he had sex in his consulting room with far more than just one patient!"

This statement was incorrect, though. (See Mandy Rice-Davies's statement – "He would, wouldn't he?")

"How the hell was I to know anything about his bloody sex life? – or care about it either?" shouted Natalie.

"Why do you think that that man dresses in such fucking loud suits that they can be heard all the way from Algeria as I said before? He dresses in that ridiculous way, to hide his previous guilt."

"Ted, I'm simply not interested in the fucking man!" said Natalie, her voice raised. She added, "all this time, I've been alone, and I haven't had the faintest idea where you've been as I said. I thought you'd been beaten up, or even murdered. There was no excuse whatever for your failure to get in touch with me. If you continue to mess me about in this way, I'm going to move in with Marigold," threatened Natalie.

"I did say I was sorry. I've only just got over a really bad attack of pneumonia. I've been seriously ill, so much so that I nearly died, after being in Intensive Care for weeks.

"There is no one, other than my children, who could have told you where I was. There are times when you can be terribly cruel, Natalie."

There was a long silence. Part of Natalie felt angry because Ted had failed to tell her where he had been. The other part of her felt sorry for him, as well as guilty.

"Tell me another thing, Natalie, do you fancy Isaac Stone?"

"No, of course, I don't, contrary to what I said earlier. He doesn't wear his tie loosened at the neck, and his trousers are loose, not nice and tight like yours. Also, he doesn't wear fabulous dark glasses in the way you do."

Ted let out a guffaw, which made Natalie feel happier. She began to massage his cock.

"I still don't feel like doing anything at the moment, as I said earlier. Was there anything at all about Stone which gave you the impression, that he fancied you?" asked Ted.

"Do we have to go on and on about that bloody man and his idiotic clothes? I don't cross-examine you about your relationship with Henrietta, whom, incidentally, I know about.

"Don't deny the fact that you've been to bed with her, because I know you have. I also heard that her boyfriend has changed the locks on their front door, to prevent you from getting into their house. Then, at a later date, you said that the locks had been changed to keep burglars out of the house. You don't tell the truth, do you?"

Ted loved jealous women. "I haven't been screwing her," he insisted adamantly.

"Bloody liar!"

"Did you love Rex Malone?" asked Ted suddenly.

"Yes. You've asked me this before."

"I know how much you loved Charlie Elliott, whose ashes I accidentally kicked over once, when I was shagging you on your living-room floor?"

Natalie flew into a rage. "You're going to get a sample of my Welsh temper, in a minute!" she shouted. "You know, perfectly well, that I loved Charlie more than any other man in the world. Don't you dare speak about him in that disrespectful way. There are some things that I simply won't tolerate and that is one of them."

"I shouldn't have said that, Nat. It's so hard for me to be perfect, sometimes, particularly when I've been very ill, as well as having lost all the money, which I worked so hard to earn. What do you think it makes me feel like, when you keep giving me money?"

"Charlie never asked me for money, and he came from a much poorer background than you did. He certainly didn't go to Eton like you," said Natalie

Ted turned off the light. Natalie had always hated the dark. She heard his silent tears. The light from the moon shone on his lovely silvery hair. Her guilt was intolerable.

Neither Natalie nor Ted slept that night. To make up for his previous boorish behaviour, he bought her a pot of tea and a pint of milk for breakfast. She felt nostalgic, because only Charlie used to bring her things to eat in bed. Ted got into bed with her and drank some of the milk hungrily.

"Tell me something, Ted. Why did you marry Belladonna?" she asked.

"I married her because she had such a sad face."

"Oh? Have you always been attracted to women with sad faces?"

"Only in her case," said Ted awkwardly.

"Do you think I've got a sad face, then?"

"No. Your face is adorable, beautiful and strong, like your lovely Welsh eyes."

"Why thank 'ee my dear!" said Natalie, trying to imitate the accent of the deep south. "Incidentally, why did you and Belladonna split up? This time, I want the truth, Ted."

"In the first place, she became useless at sex, even though she's the mother of my children. I started to take mistresses, or shall I say, I had dalliances."

"I hope you won't do that sort of thing to me. You'll be sorry if you do," said Natalie.

"No, you're a wonderful lover. I'll tell you what happened, Natalie.

"We were sitting in the garden on a hot, sunny day. I'd had two bottles of beer. Suddenly, Belladonna suddenly turned to me and asked me whether I had ever been unfaithful to her.

"Yes," I said, foolishly. "I don't claim to have been perfect all my life. I'm only human," I replied."

"I'm not perfect, either," confessed Natalie, "and I don't pretend to be. I've told dozens of lies during my life, and I've done worse things than that."

Natalie fondled his cock until it became hard, harder even than it had ever been before.

"You're a bad, bad girl!" said Ted.

"So, you actually told Belladonna the truth, did you?"

"Yes."

"You inane, bloody fool! As in the Coleridge poem, you shot the albatross, didn't you? Why the hell couldn't you have lied, like any other intelligent person?" shouted Natalie, adding, "just look at all the harm you've done to yourself!"

"I should have lied, shouldn't I? I've paid more than the price for my stupidity. Ever since that day, in the garden, the atmosphere at my home became really unpleasant, not to mention nasty. In the end I decided to move out of the house, for the sake of my sanity and that of my children. I simply couldn't bear Belladonna's vitriol and vindictiveness. There was another reason why I moved out, I was asked to treat a member of the Royal Family. Naturally, I can't say who that person was. I treated this individual for nine months, but I wasn't paid a penny for my services. Belladonna did nothing but chastise me for failing to charge the Royal."

"I think that's shocking!" said Natalie, adding, "Many members of the Royal Family, have huge properties all over the country, and apparently, not one of them pays income tax."

"When I had finished the job – that is to say – treating the Royal, I was faced with the prospect of returning to my matrimonial home (which was an anathema to me) or living in a bloody dosshouse for a few months. We all had to sleep on bunks, one on top of the other.

"The stench was terrible, and the lice got into my hair. At least, I was able to speak to some of the other people staying in the doss house. I've never been short of words, because of my profession.

"I left in the end. I went to a barber, who cleaned and cut my hair. Then, I took my filthy clothes to a dry cleaners. I was only too happy to get back to work as a psychiatrist in the hospital, I had worked in before. I also stayed in generous people's houses, helping with the cleaning and other minor duties. Most of the occupants of these houses had been patients of mine at one time or another."

Natalie was in tears again. She couldn't bear to hear about Ted's demeaning duties.

"Belladonna had lovers, including my best friend," said Ted. "She even took him to our marital bed. I came home one night after a long day's work and found them there. She herself had never done a stroke of work in her life."

"What a bitch!" shouted Natalie

The lovers had been lying side by side for more than an hour.

"What other houses have you been living in, Ted, since that tart had made it impossible for you to live in the same house, that you had lived in earlier?" asked Natalie.

"I had been staying on and off in a house in Belgravia not long ago. It was used as a disorderly house, except that it was not managed by a woman, but by a man. His name is Morgan Whitteridge. I see him from time to time. He considers *madams* to be cantankerous, vulgar and argumentative.

"He is well-known both among the art fraternity and the criminal. He is also so dangerous that even the police never go near him. He hires men as a hitmen, and often has their victims bumped off.

Ted added, "He is unusually rich but I've no idea where his money comes from. It's possible that he lives on inherited wealth. He also owns a number of Old Masters, some of which are genuine, but many are fake. He owns two or three *Van Gogh's*, which are apparently real, and which must have cost him an arm and a leg. If he ever allows you to visit his house, accompanied by me, he might show them to you, if you're polite to him."

Natalie was bored. "I don't want to see the works of that fucking schizoid hooligan. He gives me a bloody migraine!" she said angrily.

Ted laughed out loud.

"Are you interested in any works of art at all?" he asked.

"Not a lot. Except H. Bosch. Most of his work is in the *Prado* in Madrid. I can stand and gaze at his paintings for hours on end," said Natalie. "A boyfriend took me there once, and I couldn't keep my eyes off any of them."

The lovers drifted off for a while. Ted woke Natalie up after about an hour and a half.

"I do wish you'd get rid of May. She gives me the creeps. I'm afraid I'm going to have to stay in Whitteridge's house, until she leaves."

"Come on, Ted. She really is quite harmless. I've told you this before."

"In no way is she harmless. When I returned to your flat the other day, she was lying on her stomach in the hall, giggling like a bloody hyena. I can't take it anymore, Nat. I'm going to stay with Whitteridge until you get her removed. Once she's out, ring me on my mobile, to say you've got rid of her."

Ted got into a black cab. Once he arrived at Whitteridge's house, a member of the curious man's staff allocated him a basement room, free of charge. He felt rather sad to be away from Natalie, but relieved to be parted from May. He onanised every night as he thought about Natalie. He missed her so much that he couldn't stay in Whitteridge's house for long, and returned to her flat.

"I really do think you ought to have repaid this man's hospitality," said Natalie, once the two had got into bed.

She was fascinated by Ted's stories about Whitteridge, his incomprehensible lifestyle, his mysteriously earned wealth and his myriad of weird servants.

Ted delighted her by repeating the story about Whitteridge continuing to have contacts with members of the London underworld, as well as killing people in return for generous sums. There were times when she failed to believe all his stories, however.

There had been many occasions when the seemingly, bogus rogue had offered to kill Belladonna, in front of Natalie, and she had been only too enthusiastic, like a demented schoolgirl. Ted had vehemently turned all Whitteridge's offers down, however.

"Why the hell did you turn them down, you dickhead?" demanded Natalie.

"Maybe, all this is connected to *karma* in some way, although that's something I don't really understand," replied Ted. "Also, as you know, I was brought up by a clergyman, who taught me to turn the other cheek, although I ended up with no religious faith."

"Don't you realise that all your problems could be obliterated, if Belladonna were to be murdered? Nothing whatever would happen to you," said Natalie. "The woman drives a *Mini* with a short bonnet and never wears a seat belt. She is also a terrible driver, or so I've heard."

"From whom?"

"Oh, never mind."

Ted changed the subject. "I know how beautifully you write. I need your help."

"What kind of help do you need, apart from my suggestion that you have Belladonna murdered?"

"It's bloody Whitteridge who's my problem. He plays me up whenever I'm in his blasted house. He gets prostitutes in from about nine o'clock in the evening, until breakfast time the following day."

"Have you ever screwed any of these women?" asked Natalie suspiciously.

"No, of course not."

"I say that, because I have left you ten thousand pounds in my will, and if you're naughty, I'll take it away from you."

"Oh, Natalie, you are sweet! The prostitutes make such a ghastly noise when they come. The noise goes on all bloody night, and I can't sleep. Only you can stop the terrible noise."

"What the hell do you expect me to do about it?" asked Natalie in a baffled tone of voice. Besides, why can't you come and live in my flat permanently?"

"Because of that maniac. I don't know what she's going to do next." He added, "all I want you to do at the moment is write one of your brilliant, punitive letters to

Whitteridge, containing the kind of material, appearing in some of the letters, contained in many of your books. These letters are often written by your characters, when they are in a rage."

"You really are awfully long-winded," said Natalie. Can't you condense your interminable prose in any way? Of course, I'll do that for you. What will you do for me in return, though?" she added mischievously.

"You know very well what I'll do for you," said Ted.

"All right. I'll have a letter ready for you within about two hours. It will be one of my punitive letters. First, give me this man's full name and address. I know his surname is Whitteridge."

***

"I've written the letter, Ted, and I've typed it as well."
"Wonderful girl! Read it aloud."

Dear Mr Whitteridge,

Re: Unacceptably loud noises, made by prostitutes, visiting your house from nine o'clock at night, until breakfast time the following morning

The above speaks for itself. I have been informed by a psychiatrist who sometimes stays in the basement of your house, that the noise these women make on reaching orgasm, is intolerable, and that it continues throughout the night.

I must congratulate you warmly on being a most fantastic

stud, who would put even Casanova into the shade. However, I feel most strongly that your behaviour should be changed at your very earliest convenience.

The psychiatrist in question is supposed to be treating me every morning. Because of the noise made by the prostitutes, whom you employ, he is unable to sleep and wake up in time, to keep any of his appointments with me.

Hence, I have had to cancel most of these appointments, despite my having bought him a costly alarm clock.

I am not his only patient. He is also consulted by members of the Royal Family, some of whom have somewhat challenging mental health issues.

As I am a High Court Judge, and have enjoyed that rank for many years, I have the authority to close your premises down, should the loud noises made by the prostitutes when they come, continue. The police are aware and so are your singularly distressed neighbours.

Yours sincerely,

*The Honourable
Natalie Klein.*

***

Ted read the letter twice. Natalie fondled his cock at the same time.

"Is that nice?" she asked.

Ted laughed raucously and continued to laugh, until he had hiccups.

"You're a superb writer, Natalie. You only have to put pen to paper, and your ink turns to gold."

"And you're such a bloody good fuck, Ted!"

Whitteridge took Natalie's letter seriously, and actually believed that she was indeed a High Court Judge. His main weakness was that he believed whatever he was told. Not only did he silence the prostitutes who visited his house, he got rid of the lot of them.

***

Very foolishly, Ted had left a few of garments, and some Saville Row suits, in his wardrobe, in the spare bedroom, at the matrimonial home in Hampstead. Belladonna bundled all his clothes into a black plastic bag, which she threw into the back of her *Mini* in a fit of rage. Incidentally, her husband had generously given her the *Mini*, while he had been working like a dog.

She drove the car onto a dual carriageway, dragged the black, plastic bag out of the car, emptied it and dumped its contents into a field. She told her husband what she had done, and his immediate reaction was to throw an empty wine bottle at a wall, and ring Natalie.

"You really are absolutely hopeless!" she shouted. "You could easily have prevented her from doing what she did. If you weren't so phenomenally beautiful and brilliant between the sheets, I'd have told you to fuck off by now."

There was a silence. Suddenly, she felt sorry for him, as she regarded him as a gentleman.

"All right, Ted. What other garments do you need? I'll ask my chauffeur to replace them. I'm a prolific writer, as you know, and a serious woman. I haven't got time to bugger about buying men's clothes," she said, adding, "I'll tell my chauffeur to bring a tape-measure to the flat and get things done properly."

Natalie asked her chauffeur, a totally baffled Bangladeshi called Sayeed Sabur, to buy about three, navy-blue Saville Row suits, in the right size. The chauffeur arrived at her flat, tape measure in hand, and faced Natalie. Ted was finishing his breakfast. Sayeed's appearance was curious. He was wearing a round, white hat and flowing, silk robes. He stank of foul-smelling incense.

"I'm supposed to ask how a gentleman is hung," he ventured. He had read these hesitantly spoken words from a crumpled piece of paper.

"One addresses this question to the gentleman himself, not to me. I don't know anything about these matters. I'm a writer, not a tailor," said Natalie abruptly.

Sayeed moved from one foot to the other. He was ill-at-ease with the two ill-tempered Brits. Ted took a cigarette from his cigarette case and hurriedly lit it.

"Will you kindly get on with your business!" said Natalie. "You're to ask him how he is hung," she said.

Sayeed had a poor command of English and fought desperately for words.

"How many more times do I have to get you to ask a simple question?" She had no idea what she was speaking about, however.

"Could I please take your chauffeur into the bathroom?" asked Ted. "You don't understand how embarrassing you can be sometimes!"

The two men went into the bathroom, their heads lowered. Ted found Sayeed's overpowering stench of incense, intolerable and struggled to hold his bile.

Using very abrupt language, he showed Sayeed what to do, unlocked the door and opened it quickly, as if he were escaping from a fire.

When the two men had emerged from the bathroom, Natalie asked her employee to sit on one of the sofas, produced an A4 sheet of paper and wrote instructions in block capitals about her lover's wardrobe.

She asked to Sayeed to go to a top men's shop and buy three Savile Row suits, navy in colour, at least four pairs of particularly tight-fitting, navy blue jeans, a number of white shirts, open at the neck, three matching ties, and two navy blue blazers. Navy blue was Ted's favourite colour.

She ordered a few navy-blue cashmere sweaters, at least ten navy blue socks, and easy fitting shoes of the same colour.

"The gentleman also needs a five-hundred-pound wristwatch, as he's lost his original watch, blast it!" ordered Natalie.

The bill for these items was enormous, but she failed to tell Ted exactly what it amounted to, for fear of humiliating him.

"You're an absolute brick, Nat!" he said. He often uttered these words which, ironically, were Charlie's words as well.

"You say that a lot, don't you, sexpot," replied Natalie. "You'd better watch it, though. I'm a very good friend, but I'm also a horrible enemy. Cross my path and you'll wish you'd never been born!"

"I know," replied Ted, "I certainly wouldn't want to get on the wrong side of you!" He continued to adore her and fear her at the same time. "I'd never do that, Nat. You're too dear to me," he said.

The lovers were in bed once more in Natalie's flat, following the sex act.

"I've got a suggestion to make," said Natalie

"What suggestion?"

"I know I'm repeating myself, but you told me recently that Belladonna owned a *Mini*, which is effectively a coffin on wheels, because of its short bonnet. You also told me that she had an aversion to seat belts, as well as being an erratic and very dangerous driver."

"Oh God, not that one again!" said Ted.

"Is her life insured?"

"I understand what you're saying, Natalie, but the answer is "No". Just as it was when we discussed this tedious matter before."

"Come on, Ted. What I suggest we do is in the interests of what is right as I said before. Can't I make you change your mind?"

"No, Natalie, no! Christ! You're like bloody Lady Macbeth!" said Ted.

"God, you're wet!" exclaimed Natalie.

***

It was sunny the following day. Ted went for a walk and Natalie began to write again. She then rang Stone, and told his receptionist that she was in urgent need of storage space for her lover's suits and other garments. She asked the receptionist to arrange for these things to be stored in Stone's consulting room, in a black, plastic bag. The receptionist put her call through to Stone.

"Hullo, Dr Stone. This is Natalie." She explained Ted's dilemma and also told the puzzled, strangely clad psychiatrist about his rival's wife's vicious act of throwing all his clothes into a field. She chose her words as carefully as she could, and added that the woman was totally evil.

"I know you've got a very large consulting-room. Is there any chance of my storing Dr Curruthers' clothing somewhere on your premises?"

Stone was outraged.

"In no way am I going to store Dr Curruthers' clothes in my consulting room, or indeed in any other part of the building!" he said, his voice raised, "Tell him to store his blasted bloody clothes in lockers at Waterloo Station!"

"Have you no compassion, Dr Stone. Have you none of the milk of human kindness?" asked Natalie. "You are a psychiatrist, are you not? Psychiatrists are supposed to have kind hearts," she added banally.

Stone put the phone down. Natalie rang him again and showered invective at him.

"Have you found somewhere for me to store the clothes you so generously bought for me?" Ted asked Natalie. They were in a pub in Victoria Street, and had had quite a lot to drink.

"If you really want to know, I rang up your dear friend, Dr Isaac Stone, and asked him if he would be prepared to store your clothes in his consulting room."

"W-H-A-A-T?"

"You heard me."

"Did you really ask him to do that, Nat?"

"Yes, of course, I did. It's time the bastard learned some elementary humanity."

"I can't tell you how much embarrassment you've caused me," said Ted mildly.

***

Ted made his way to Waterloo station, using the London Underground. He found the lockers, and clumsily stuffed as many articles of clothing as he could into the lockers. He kept the plastic bag with him and returned to his lover's flat later that night. While the two were in bed, Natalie noticed that her lover wasn't wearing the five-hundred-pound wristwatch which she had given him.

"What the hell's happened to your watch, Ted?"

"I'm afraid I've had to pawn it, Nat. I'd had nothing to eat for three days. Even the food banks were empty. As I said many times, Belladonna has genuinely prevented me from earning my living, and even from having a square meal," confessed Ted.

"I will never forgive you for pawning the watch I gave you. It cost me five-hundred pounds! You have shown no respect for me at all," Natalie bellowed, adding, "I want you out of here now. Dr Stone has told me I can share his bed.

Ted took the plastic bag from the spare room, dressed slowly and left the flat. His cheeks were tear stained. He planned to ask Whitteridge for board and lodging once more. It didn't occur to him to beg Natalie to go back on her word. He was too proud.

It is true that Natalie had been very cruel to Ted, although he really had no means of earning any money. Natalie had hurt him but only on a spontaneous basis. She would not have flown into such a rage, had she fully understood her lover's words about the loss of the watch.

Because of the operation Ted had had to undergo in the past, his left arm was malfunctioning, as he had once explained to his lover, and a very small part of his brain was damaged. He could not even get a job as a driver, as he had too many points on his licence.

It was also impossible for him to go onto benefits, because of what he described as an interminable waiting list. He could not do anything at all, even in 2020s Britain. He had fallen through a net, which was not entirely of his own creation. He ate from dustbins, whenever he could, and slept side by side with dossers, sometimes under arches and other times in doorways. He was too proud to beg from passers-by. Natalie had no real idea of his plight at this time.

***

Natalie and Dr Stone had become lovers, although Dr Stone was not nearly as attractive or as accomplished a lover as Ted. They were walking down Victoria Street, with their arms linked, like husband and wife. Stone was crudely dressed as usual. Natalie was wearing a black leather suit and high-heeled shoes. She had made a considerable amount of money, following the sale of one of her best-selling books.

The couple were about to cross the road. Suddenly, a faint sound could be heard. Natalie heard someone calling her name. She heard the noise once more, and then a third time.

Ted was dressed very shabbily, but in Natalie's opinion quite attractively. He was leaning against a doorway. The first thing Natalie saw was his beautiful, silvery hair. She could only just make out the outline of his face. Though still beautiful, his cheeks were whitish, and his jagged white teeth shone in the light of the moon. The remainder of his crumpled attire had still been stored at Waterloo Station.

"Ted!" Natalie called out.

Stone swung round. He recognised his beautiful rival straight away and hated him.

"I don't think we've met," Stone said unpleasantly. He realised that he was in a triangular situation, and walked away, leaving Natalie and Ted behind.

Natalie eased Ted to his feet. He was not clean enough to go to her flat, so she took him to the nearest public bath house, which was still open. He staggered into a cubicle, dragged his clothes off and washed himself three times, because there wasn't any soap available. Natalie dried him, pulled on his vest and briefs, and helped him to walk to her *Ford Focus*. She drove him to Waterloo Station, so that he could collect the remainder of his clothes.

Ted had forgotten the whereabouts of his keys to the lockers storing his clothes. Finally, the Senior Station

Manager came on duty. He recognised Natalie from her photographs, which had appeared on the backs of her books.

The Manager was pleasant and sympathetic. He was able to produce some of the keys to the lockers, after a long search. Ted removed his underwear, threw it onto the floor, and managed to put on one of his fractionally smarter suits. Although the suit was extremely creased, his appearance was not completely unacceptable. Natalie helped him to pull his other suits out of the lockers, and stuffed them into the bag he had with him.

He was very shivery, so Natalie took him to a steak house in Victoria Street. He wolfed down a slab of steak, as if he had never eaten anything in his life before. He asked for another, as well as two bottles of red wine. He then ordered some chocolate cake, covered with ice cream. The colour returned to his cheeks, after he had eaten.

"What have you been doing since you left my flat?" asked Natalie tactlessly, once they arrived home.

"Dossing, mostly. I didn't want to come back to the flat, once you'd thrown me out. I was much too proud to do that. I went to Whitteridge's house, hoping he'd be able to put me up, but the place seemed empty. I knocked on the front door, over and over again, and in the end, the butler opened it.

""Yes?" he said. He was drunk and his speech was slurred.

"He told me that Whitteridge had been arrested for having had someone murdered. The defendant had appeared at the Old Bailey, and was found guilty of murder. In the end, he was given thirty years."

Natalie was stunned. She wondered what would have happened, had she had Belladonna murdered. Her eyes filled with tears.

"What prison was Whitteridge sent to?" she asked eventually.

"Wormwood Scrubs."

Natalie went out of her way to amuse Ted. "I know that prison," she began. "I applied for a job there, teaching prisoners to read and write.

"The governor interviewed me in his plush office which had family photographs covering the walls. I thought I was getting on brilliantly.

"Not so, I was sent a short letter, saying that my request had been turned down."

"Why was it turned down?" asked Ted.

"Dogged does it, has always been my motto!" said Natalie. "I asked the governor over and over again, why I had been turned down.

"In the end, he reluctantly rang me back, and said, "We regret that we found you exceptionally unfit. You were unable to mount a very small flight of steps, without being able to hold the railings with both hands, and when you eventually managed to get to the top, you were far too exhausted to speak!"

"What the hell has this got to do with reading and writing?" asked Ted, who laughed gleefully.

Natalie was overjoyed by his laughter, and by the fact that she had found him again, after having been so cruel to him.

"You really do strike me as being terribly slow on your feet," said Ted. "I noticed this when I first met you, after your father had fainted in the South of France that time. You were in a terrible state. You walked across my consulting room like a sedated fly."

"Thanks a lot, Ted," said Natalie. My father had fainted in the south of France. I thought he was dead. It was a sight which made me freak out!"

After the lovers had finished their conversation about Natalie's slow gait, they left the flat and went to a different pub this time. Ted had a double whisky, and Natalie had three double gin and tonics. They walked slowly towards Natalie's *Ford Focus*. Her whole being was saturated with relief.

Despite the three gin and tonics, she was still able to drive Ted back to her flat. Then she shaved him and put him to bed, with the electric blanket on. She made him a pot of Yorkshire tea, his and her favourite. He drank the whole pot, followed by another. She promised him she would ask Sayeed to buy him more clothes the following day, to replace the ones in storage at Waterloo Station, which were no longer in an acceptable condition.

She rang Dr Festenstein and begged him to come to her flat and give her lover a check-up to make up for his rough living. Fortunately, he couldn't find anything wrong with his patient, but he urged Ted to cut down his smoking.

She paid Dr Festenstein, waited until he had left, and took Ted's hands in hers.

"I'm so terribly, terribly sorry, Ted," she said. "Please don't think anything more about the watch. I was in a rage. Not only that, I was unnecessarily cruel to you."

"True love means not having to say how sorry you are all the time," replied Ted.

"I'm sorry about Whitteridge," she added, "but don't worry, I'll think of another way to punish the whore. I'll punish her if it's the last thing I do."

"Oh, not her again, for mercy's sake!" said Ted, "you really can be awfully boring."

***

The pair continued to meet in Natalie's flat on Tuesday afternoons, but May, Natalie's maid, was becoming increasingly batty, as her illness worsened.

May had worked for Natalie for several years, and was devoted to her boss. Natalie, too, was fond of May, and confided in her, despite her increasing disability.

May's new doctor insisted that his patient take her pills every morning, without fail. When she obeyed him, her behaviour and speech were normal, and she could hold her own in any conversation or argument. If she failed to take her pills, however, her terrifying symptoms returned and were even worse than before.

Natalie was worried sick by May's doctor's diagnoses, namely that her dementia was worsening, as the months passed by, pills or no pills. Ted was still very much in awe of her, despite the fact that he was a psychiatrist, who should have been able to deal appropriately, with anyone who did not enjoy robust mental health.

It was May's increasingly frightening appearance which really unsettled Ted, more than a rabid tiger. Her uncombed hair was even wilder than it had been earlier, and her wide eyes still bordered on the terrifyingly insane.

As Ted was continuing to visit Natalie every Tuesday, it was up to Natalie to explain May's ever-worsening disability to him, without alarming him too much.

She didn't really understand the true nature of dementia, and became almost as terrified of her as Ted was.

He had had experiences in almost every psychiatric hospital, in and outside London, and in Harley Street as well. It was there that severely mentally ill patients crossed the Atlantic to seek his advice. His experiences were not only related to England, but to other continents. Despite his fear of May's vile appearance, he was painfully reminded, not only of the evil Belladonna, but also, of Mr Rochester's incarcerated wife in Charlotte Bronte's novel, *Jane Eyre*. This novel was one of Natalie's favourites.

Natalie took her lover to the dining-room at the Ritz, as she knew its ambience would put him at his ease.

"About May, Ted," she ventured casually, as the menu was being passed round the table, "you simply must understand that she is quite harmless, as I've told you repeatedly. I know her appearance is somewhat eccentric, as is her behaviour, but I don't really think she'd be capable of hurting a fly. She has to take certain pills every day, as you know. Provided she does so, she is as normal as you or I."

"That's not what the residents in your building have said," remarked Ted cynically.

"I know what happened," said Natalie impatiently. "I saw May going outside the building, stark naked, and talking to a parked *Mini*."

"Don't you think that going outside a building, naked, and talking to a parked car, is a bit rum?" asked Ted mildly. He put a thick lump of butter onto his toast.

"I suppose it would have been much more appropriate, if she had been talking to a *Rolls-Royce* instead," replied Natalie, "and I told her so."

Natalie had amused Ted once more. His fear of May's horrifying appearance and behaviour had temporarily disappeared. He returned to Natalie's flat the following Tuesday.

This time, Natalie made sure that May had taken her pills that morning. She waited for her to appear calm, and sat her down on one of the sofas. She poured her a glass of sherry, although her doctor had forbidden her to drink alcohol.

"It's very nice weather, isn't it, May?" ventured Natalie, her voice was trembling.

"Oh, yes, yes, indeed."

"You did take your pills this morning, didn't you?"

"Oh, aye. I think I did."

"Either you took them, or you didn't take them, May?"

"I'm sure I took them."

"That's my girl."

"Now, you and I will go through the rules about the gentleman's visit today at five o'clock."

"What gentleman?"

"The psychiatrist."

"What's a psychiatrist?"

"Never mind, May, never mind! He's just a friend of mine. You don't need to know exactly who he is."

"Eh?"

"I'm now going to have a quick word with you about the bed in your room."

"Oh, yes, the bed."

"Now, you know that there are two beds in your room, one which you sleep in every night, and the other one, which is empty. That means there isn't anyone in it. Could I ask you to make the empty bed, please? You do know how to make a bed, don't you?"

"Oh, aye."

"Just before five o'clock, I will unlock your door, and I will remove the key. Then you must go downstairs, and hand the key to the hall porter. Stay with him and chat to him, but do not, in any circumstances whatever, return to this flat, until eight o'clock tonight. I have already given these instructions to the hall porter."

"Oh, aye."

Ted arrived at Natalie's flat at five o'clock, went into the bathroom and washed his hands.

"Hello, sexy!" said Natalie. He was wearing his tie loosened at the neck, and his trousers were tight-fitting. (This was her fetish.) He was also wearing dark glasses, which turned her on like a light. She grabbed him by the crotch, and he became hard straight away.

Natalie led him to the bedroom with twin beds where they had violent sex. Neither of them noticed May, who was occupying her own bed. This was not the first time she had done this.

***

The following day, May appeared to have deteriorated further, so Natalie took her to see Dr Festenstein, who said he would arrange for the unfortunate woman to have various tests performed.

"I'm devoted to May," began Natalie, with tears in her eyes, "but Ted's scared stiff of her. There must be something you can do for her. Otherwise, we will both have to go to a hotel, and send the bill to May's relatives."

Dr Festenstein went through a battery of examinations. He also asked his patient to repeat words and numbers, and to count backwards.

May remained in his consulting room for at least an hour, and did her best to answer his questions, most of which she found very difficult.

"What's wrong with her? Isn't there anything you can do to get her right?" pleaded Natalie.

"My dearest Natalie, as you know, I can refuse you nothing, but there really isn't anything I can do to help May. She has dementia, which can only get worse, not better. In the end, she will die.

"At first, her illness can be kept at bay with certain pills, which will not last for more than about six months, if that. By this time, she will cease to recognise, even her nearest and dearest," Dr Festenstein continued,

"Sometimes, she will be able to walk along pavements in the street. Other times, she could easily wander into the road, and might well be knocked over by oncoming traffic, which could kill her."

"What should I do? I can't put her into a home. That would be too cruel," said Natalie.

"Does she have any relatives?" asked Dr Festenstein.

"She has two daughters, I think. One is quite pleasant. The other is very uncooperative, though. My only hope is that the nice daughter might be prepared to give May a helping hand," said Natalie, adding, "I really can't have a raving madwoman breathing into my face, when I'm in the middle of a fuck!"

Dr Festenstein cleared his throat. "You do have a singularly black sense of humour!" he said at length.

"I bloody well need it, after all the trauma I've had to put up with. Black humour is the only thing I've got left to keep my head above water!"

"I only hope May will be able to get some help from the nicer of her daughters," said Dr Festenstein. "Ring me any time you need me."

***

Before May was handed over to the most caring of her two daughters, she approached Natalie at three o'clock one morning, while she was trying to beat a publisher's deadline. She was fully clothed and was brandishing a carving knife, which was stroking Natalie's neck.

"Who the hell are you?" asked May obscurely.

"I'm Natalie bloody Klein, and I'm your fucking boss!" said Natalie. "What the hell are you doing with that carving knife in your hand, touching my neck?"

"I was just looking for some cheese in the fridge."

"Have you ever seen cheese growing out of someone's neck?" asked Natalie mildly.

Strangely, she was unafraid at the time. Her immediate reaction was to dress, hire a minicab and make her way to the nearest police station. She told the driver to wait for her outside.

The policeman she approached was junior in rank and was pretty disinterested in her case.

"My maid has just approached me with a carving knife in her hand," said Natalie. She gave the policeman her name and address, and stated that she was a prolific writer, who was trying to meet a publisher's deadline.

"I require twenty-four-hour police protection," she stated. "I am at risk of being stabbed to death by this woman who is mentally disturbed."

The policeman was uncooperative and was playing *Patience*. Natalie was angry and impatient and commented that all the police ever did was break into people's houses, looking for cannabis, at the taxpayers' expense.

"Oh, piss off, you silly, old boot!" said the policeman.

"I'll take your name and that of your Chief Superintendent, with intent to have you relieved of your responsibilities," barked Natalie.

The policeman continued to play *Patience* and did nothing.

Natalie asked the minicab driver, to take her to the house, owned by her nephew, Jeremy Nathaniel Klein, who lived with his wife and four children in Fulham. Jeremy was very close to Natalie. He had nearly died in infancy, which had caused her to adore him throughout his life.

Jeremy was incensed by the manner, in which his distinguished, but very eccentric aunt, had been treated by the police. He did not dress, and got into the minicab, wearing pyjamas, a dressing-gown and a pair of slippers. Natalie accompanied him, and asked the driver to go to the same police station as the one his aunt had been to.

He spoke to the same policeman, who was surprised by his bizarre apparel.

"My name is Jeremy Nathaniel Klein," he began, "I am third in line to Mr Selwyn Klein, who owns the *Klein Newspaper Group*.

"You were rude enough to address my aunt, Miss Natalie Klein, author of a series of books, as 'you silly old boot', when she told you that her maid had approached her, brandishing a carving knife, without provocation. Is this true?"

"Well, err, yes, sir," stuttered the policeman, adding, "I'd had a very long day."

"The length of your day makes no difference to me whatever. I'll take your name," said Jeremy.

"John Dibbs, sir."

"I'm reporting you to your Chief Superintendent. My aunt also asked to speak to your Chief Superintendent, but to no avail."

"I'm sorry, sir."

"So am I. You will be hearing from my family again."

***

It was four o'clock the following morning, and Ted was sleeping with Natalie once more. May was staying with her favourite daughter. Natalie heard a woman's voice on the phone. It was loud and carrying.

"Can you please come over, Ted. I'm suicidal. I've decided to jump off the roof."

"Don't do anything until I come to your house, Henrietta. I'll be there in about twenty minutes' time."

"I've heard Henrietta's name being mentioned, more than once," said Natalie. "Who is she?"

"She's an ex-patient of mine. I forgot to turn off my mobile. Also, she's just threatened to kill herself, by jumping off the roof of her house."

"A likely story!" said Natalie. "If I hear you've been screwing her, I'll cut you out of my will. I've said this many times before, haven't I?"

"I haven't been screwing her, damn it," said Ted.

He returned to Natalie's flat within two hours. He lay on his back with his hands crossing his chest, like a medieval saint. He was asleep.

Natalie, though extremely suspicious, licked his hands. He woke up with a start.

"Were you dreaming that Henrietta was doing this to you?" she asked.

"No." He giggled but he was beginning to feel henpecked. He was exhausted.

"Are you likely to see Henrietta again?"

"Not if I can help it."

"Why did you say that?"

"Because her boyfriend has changed the bloody locks."

"I've heard that one before. Did he change the locks to prevent you from coming into her house again?" asked Natalie.

"I have no intention of going anywhere near her blasted, bloody house. He changed them because he was afraid of burglars. There have been quite a few burglars in the area," said Ted abruptly.

"You know the rules, don't you, Ted, about my will."

"Of course, I do, Nat. Why the hell do you think I'd want to deceive you?"

"Because you deceived Belladonna, didn't you, when you spoke to her on that hot, sunny day?"

"Oh, please, Nat, that was such a long time ago," said Ted. "Besides, I really have improved my behaviour since then. Belladonna was frigid and evil. You are definitely neither of those things. In fact, you're the hottest lover I've ever had in my life."

"Don't push your luck, Ted, as I said before," said Natalie, adding, "I'm not a very nice enemy."

Ted would never have cared to deceive her. He adored Natalie, more than any other woman he had slept with in his life.

The lovers had violent sex.

***

Within about three days, Jeremy Klein, Natalie, Ted, May, two surgeons, one neurologist, and a GP, assembled, accompanied by the Senior Trustee of the Klein Group. Also, Mrs Jane Smith, who managed Natalie's taxes and royalty statements, all took their places at a plush leather conference table in the Klein offices.

Dr Festenstein was there as well. He was wearing a monogrammed tie and *Gucci* shoes. Everybody was impeccably dressed, except for May, who was wearing soiled, frayed blue jeans and a torn T-shirt, covered with food stains.

Selwyn Klein was not there, however. That day, he put time aside to plant trees in his wood near his Buckinghamshire house. Apart from journalism, planting trees was his passion.

Besides, he didn't fancy speaking about mentally disturbed maids, a subject which depressed him. Natalie's other brothers felt the same way, and it was only Jeremy who actually liked dealing with such matters. There was an old-fashioned tape recorder on the table.

Jeremy, who was immaculately dressed, rose to his feet and addressed May, who looked more like a tramp than a maid.

"I'm very distressed indeed to have to speak to you in this manner, May, as, over the years, my aunt has felt very affectionately towards you, and more than happy with your services. However, because of your singularly dangerous behaviour of late, it will no longer be appropriate for you to remain in my aunt's employ.

"I will take these points in turn:

1. You started a fire by turning a radiator on upside-down. This could easily have caused the building, in which you have been working, to burst into flames.
2. You threw your clothes onto the floor, as well as a lit cigarette. Likewise, this could have had the same effect.
3. You approached my aunt in the small hours of the morning, brandishing a carving knife, while she was trying to meet her publisher's deadline, terrifying her out of her wits.

To excuse yourself, you said you had been using the knife to help yourself to some cheese from the fridge.

When my aunt asked you whether you expected to find cheese growing out of her neck, where you were trying to plunge the knife, you accused my aunt of persecuting you. You then threatened to sue her for defamation of character.

4. You are having a severely detrimental effect on my aunt's writing career, as well as her relationship with her publisher.
5. You also caused my aunt embarrassment when you removed all your clothes, in the lobby of the building you occupy, went outside and spoke at length to a parked car. You greatly disturbed my aunt's neighbours on this occasion.
6. Last but not least, when my aunt was engaging in sexual activity, with a highly respectable gentleman, you leant over her face and asked her where your radio was. You then tapped the gentleman on the shoulder, and demanded that he stop whatever he was doing, get out of bed immediately, and institute a thorough search for the radio himself, because you wished to listen to *The Archers*.

(Jeremy found it hard to keep a straight face at this point.)

May flew into a rage. "You're telling a pack of lies, Mr Klein. I intend to consult my solicitor. You are rubbish!"

"I'm afraid things are way beyond that, May," said Jeremy. "Everybody at this table, except your own good self, is adamant that, you suffer from dementia. Your daughter is staying near the flat you have been occupying. She is going to help you to pack your bags, and look after you until a suitable home can be found for you."

Jeremy added, "I think this concludes the meeting. However, we must all thank you May, for your great kindness towards my aunt, over the years." May suddenly gesticulated, swore, kicked and completely lost control of herself. Jeremy remained calm.

"Andy, the doorman, will show you out of the building, and into a car, where your daughter will be waiting for you," said Jeremy, adding, "Thank you, for everything, May. My aunt has really appreciated your kindness. Good luck."

May pushed some blotting paper and pens off the table. She also picked up a paperknife and threw it violently against one of the walls.

"You'll be hearing from me again!" she shouted. "I'm taking you all to court." She stormed out of the room, slamming the door behind her.

Natalie went over to where Jeremy had been sitting, and told him how impressed she had been by his legalistic speech, releasing May from her employ. She said how sorry she was about her maid's expulsion, though, and suggested that everybody go out to lunch. Jeremy said he would be more than happy to do so, to celebrate Natalie's liberation.

"I'd like to introduce you to my dear friend, Ted Curruthers," said Natalie. "He and I are going out together. He has recently divorced his wife. Her name is Belladonna, and she has been exceptionally cruel to him. She gave him such a horrible time that he was once on the verge of taking his life. Mercifully, I prevented such a ghastly tragedy from taking place."

"I know Ted, well," Jeremy told Natalie at lunch. "We went to school together. He married an evil woman who ruined his life, and took all his money. I know all about her."

Jeremy continued, this time in a rage, which was rare for this mild, gentle young man.

"I've found out worse things about Belladonna. Ted, though bereft of the things which meant so much to him, had been losing all his friends, one by one.

"This was engineered by the conniving behaviour of Belladonna. She managed to get Ted's closest friends together and, even to go so far as to drag them into the matrimonial bed, one by one.

"There were worse things than that on Belladonna's hate list, but I certainly would not wish to list them," said Jeremy.

"I know the lot. It was I who hired a private dick!" said Natalie proudly.

Jeremy changed the subject.

"Incidentally, I'd like you to feel welcome to the Klein family, and we are happy to offer you all the friendship we can give you. If you need anything, let me know."

Ted was touched. He and Jeremy embraced.

After lunch, Ted felt like a new person. He had eaten a square meal for a change. For the first time, Natalie trusted him completely. They did not plan to get married, because of Natalie's remaining love for Charlie, and her refusal to change her surname. She had always been very possessive about her surname.

She hired a decent cook, as well as a competent cleaner,

called Hetty. Sometimes, Ted and Natalie bickered a little, but, on the whole, they got on well.

"Have you ever wanted children?" asked Ted at dinner on one occasion.

"No, my books are my children," Natalie replied.

***

Jeremy often came to dinner in Natalie's flat, which was cooked by Anne, the new cook. Ted invariably wolfed down three courses and felt much better than he had felt when he was fed by Belladonna. After dinner one evening, Jeremy and Ted played chess, while Natalie went upstairs and wrote at length before watching a horror film.

The men had been playing chess on another occasion, and Jeremy was winning. He was a good player, whereas Ted was not.

"There's something I think I should tell you, Ted," said Jeremy one evening.

"Oh, yes?"

"It's about your smoking. You smoke far, far too much."

"Natalie thinks it's sexy," said Ted.

"How many do you smoke a day?"

"Oh, God knows."

"Can't you cut it down? I know it will cause you lung cancer one day. Do you want to get lung cancer?"

Ted looked very depressed.

"I couldn't give a fuck!" he said.

Ted was in better spirits the following day. Jeremy

took him to *White's Men's Club* for lunch, before going to his offices. During the afternoon, Ted returned to Natalie's flat, and immersed himself in many of her books, while she went to the cinema. She saw the film, *The Death of Stalin*, and found it so funny that she was falling all over the cinema, she was laughing so much.

Stalin spoke with a crude, Yorkshire accent. Beria spoke with a Yiddish accent and Khrushchev had an accent of the deep south. At one point, Beria and Khrushchev danced in slow motion! Natalie always referred to Beria as "Bright Button Beriwinkle."

When the time came for Beria to be executed, the comical and ridiculous-looking man ran up and downstairs, and finally ended up in a lavatory.

"You can't execute me in here, comrades, this is a lavatory!" he shouted.

Ted, Jeremy and Natalie, had dinner at eight o'clock. Jeremy's children had grown up by this time, and dined with their mother. Natalie described the film she had seen, and told the men how hilarious she had found it.

Ted didn't hesitate to tell Jeremy the pleasure that some of Natalie's books had given him. Naturally, Natalie, who was exceptionally vain, was flattered.

"Shall we play chess later?" asked Jeremy.

"I'm not all that good, as you know, I'm afraid," said Ted modestly, "but I'll certainly play with you, provided you allow me to cheat with my knights, and take your Queen off the board, whenever I feel like it."

"You're really quite a rogue, aren't you, Ted?" said Jeremy, "but please, for Natalie's sake, cut down the fags.

"You must think of her. She's had a terrible bereavement. When she lost her beloved Charlie, she nearly died. Do you realise that she tried to commit suicide and was very nearly successful?" said Jeremy.

"She just can't tolerate bereavements. She's as tough as an old boot, but bereavement is something she can't handle."

"Don't you know that Sir Winston Churchill smoked dozens of cigars and lived until he was ninety," said Ted.

"All I'm asking you to do is to stop being so inconsiderate," said Jeremy. "Natalie loves you more than she can say in words. She's done so much for you. She's even stopped you from killing yourself, when you rang her up and said you were going to do so, once."

"I'll try. God knows, I'll try!" repeated Ted. "I bow my head in shame."

When Jeremy was looking the other way, Ted smiled mischievously, moved one of his Knights sideways, and sideways once more. He then took his opponent's Queen off the board.

"Checkmate, you filthy cheat!" said Jeremy angrily. "Also, it's time you cleaned up this room and emptied the ashtrays, instead of leaving everything to Natalie, who has all her books to write. You really are a proverbial slob!"

Natalie and the two men stayed in her flat, for about a month. Sometimes, they went out to dinner together. Ted saw to it that he got all his papers in order, and eventually managed to find two rooms in Harley Street.

Although, he wasn't allowed to prescribe medicine anymore, he was able to lecture students and practice psychology. He frequently helped students with their medical research as well, and, at first, he felt fulfilled.

He left Natalie's flat for a short period of time during the day, and returned most evenings. Jeremy continued to stay for dinner.

While he was working in Harley Street, Ted sometimes left the building, and smoked a lot of cigarettes in the street. It did not take him many months for his lungs to deteriorate dramatically. By the time at least ten months had passed, nearly half of one of his lungs had almost wasted away.

As he could no longer prescribe pills, he gradually felt desperately sad. Despite the fact that he was unable to use prescription pads, he began to miss the lovely house and garden he had lived in in Hampstead and had loved so much.

Gradually, he became severely depressed and no longer cared about the deterioration of his lungs, which had become even worse than they had been before. Natalie knew how ill he was, but even the sex which she provided regularly, did little to lift his melancholia.

He consulted a chest physician in Harley Street, who told him that one of his lungs was no longer in use. When he finally told Natalie the news, he broke her heart, and she couldn't stop crying. A surgeon, a colleague of Dr Festenstein, was summoned to the flat. Natalie knew him well and considered him to be very obliging.

The following evening, Ted asked Natalie to ring for an ambulance, which took almost an hour to arrive. Natalie shovelled some *diazepam* down her throat. The lovers finally got into the ambulance. After an ambulance worker had carried Ted into the ambulance on a stretcher, and put an oxygen mask over his face, but, even though traffic conditions were pretty reasonable that evening, the ambulance driver moved unacceptably slowly, and even failed to sound the siren, despite Ted's terrible illness.

Natalie slapped his face, as hard as she possibly could.

"Sound the bloody siren, for Christ sake! My boyfriend is dying!"

"Are you trying to teach me how to do my job?" asked the driver disagreeably.

"Only when you seem unable to do it yourself. Do you want me to drive your ambulance for you?"

Ted was admitted to a ward, and Natalie insisted on accompanying him, and more sophisticated x-rays were performed by yet another surgeon who, on coming into Ted's cubicle said,

"Sir, I have tragic news."

"Oh, what's news?"

"You've got terminal cancer in both lungs."

Ted frenziedly reached for a cigarette, because he didn't care anymore. Natalie knew that Belladonna was responsible for Ted's compulsive smoking, and she made up her mind that she would kill her once he had died, and turn the gun on herself.

Jeremy stopped working, once Natalie had told him the sad news. Ted no longer had medical insurance and spent all his time lying on a National Health bed, breathing in gasps. The ward was dark and bleak. Jeremy and Natalie spent all their time on either side of Ted's bed, each one holding one of his hands.

"I want you to promise me one thing, Natalie," said Ted between gasps.

"Yes?"

"Will you promise me you won't harm Belladonna?"

Jeremy came onto the ward, shortly.

"Jeremy, will you promise never to harm Belladonna?" asked Ted.

"How can I possibly promise not to do that? Don't you remember all those times, when I said I knew the difference between right and wrong, and good and evil?" said Jeremy.

Ted had become deaf, because of the tension troubling him.

"What about you, Jeremy? Will you promise not to harm her?"

"I'm not going to promise anything," said Jeremy.

One of the nurses told Jeremy and Natalie that it was time for them to leave the ward. Just as they were about to do so, Belladonna flounced onto the ward, her eyes full of hate.

She bent over the dying Ted, and cackled raucously. "I'm glad I cuckolded you!" she shouted. Natalie returned her look of hatred, and spat in her face.

Ted ignored Belladonna. "Don't worry, Nat. Ted will be here in the morning," he assured her, talking in the third person.

When she returned the following morning, he was dead.

Ted Curruthers' funeral was due to take place in Saint Joseph's Church, where his daughter, Cindy, was expected to be married.

Belladonna was dressed shabbily in brown and occupied the front pew. She was sitting in the aisle, and was expecting, hypocritically, to be able to make a speech during the ceremony sometime. Her son, Eddie, snatched the pamphlet from her hand. Although her face was pale, and devoid of tears, Ted's children, Cindy and Eddie, wept profusely. Neither child glanced at Belladonna.

A vicar entered the church, followed by a massive congregation, full to the point of overflowing. Its occupants comprised, not only practically most members of the medical profession, in and outside London, but a myriad of Ted's closest friends, and members of his family, all of whom despised Belladonna. Her sister Livia had failed to turn up.

Natalie and Jeremy, neither looking particularly conspicuous, were among the congregation. Both sat down at the back on either side of the aisle. Natalie was carrying a large white wreath, under her arm. It was hiding a ladies' *Smith and Wesson* revolver. Jeremy noticed that she was carrying a gun, and tried to ease it from her hand.

The coffin, which looked simple, was brought to the front of the church. Natalie couldn't control her tears. She had taken yet another dose of *Diazepam* to calm her nerves.

She and Jeremy walked through the crowd of mourners towards the front pew, where Belladonna was getting ready to make her bogus speech.

Natalie placed her wreath in front of the coffin, raised her revolver, and pointed it between her enemy's eyes. The *Diazepam* had steadied her shaking hand.

Belladonna inadvertently dropped her notes and bent over to pick them up. Natalie was the first to catch her eye: "Slut! Murderer! Prostitute!" Some members of the congregation were aghast.

Jeremy bound towards his tempestuous aunt. "Do you want me to visit my batty old aunt in Holloway, you maniac?" He finally managed to take the gun from her hand. This, he did, with a considerable effort.

Natalie felt an even greater surge of love for Jeremy. "I'd swing for you, my boy," she said, and squeezed his hand as firmly as she could.

As for Belladonna, she had seen the revolver and was terrified of Natalie. She ran from the church, towards a damp bedsit, which she had arranged to stay in indefinitely. She bitterly regretted the self-inflicted sadness of her life, combined with her cruelty towards her benevolent husband. She sank into an un-lifting state of melancholia, which stayed with her until she was laid in earth.

***

Natalie was asked to appear in Court, due to her possession of a firearm.

"Is it true that you bought Dr Curruthers a car on one occasion, in the distant past?" asked her cross-examining barrister.

"Yes."

"Why?" asked the barrister in a baffled tone of voice.

"Christ, sir, I needed his cock inside me, didn't I?" shouted Natalie vulgarly.

The judge cleared his throat. "Dashed expensive cock, what!" he muttered eventually.